PUBLIC WORKS

NEIL HAGERTY

PUBLIC WORKS

DRAG CITY | 2004 | CHICAGO

DRAG CITY INC., ATTN: PERMISSIONS DEPARTMENT
P.O. BOX 476867, CHICAGO, IL 60647-6867

Drag City web address: www.dragcity.com
Neil Hagerty web address: www.howlinghex.com

Printed in the United States of America

Library of Congress Control Number: 2004112413
ISBN: 0-9656183-8-2

First Edition

Cover illustration by Neil Hagerty
Back cover photo by xxx

I

JAMES CLARE

James realized the sun was red so he asked at the post office and they explained to him wildfires were burning in the valley ten miles beyond the mountain. The sky was filled with smoke and the oaks stood stark against it with darkened veins and paled winter surfaces.

A pair of bulls battled in the fields near the road as he drove home. They faced each other, horns interlocked and necks angled downward. They might have stayed that way for hours ceding or annexing space inch-by-inch. A cow looked on, her hide the exact shade of the sun-worn leather seats of his car.

James reached across the car seat as he drove home and rummaged through the mail with his fingertips—not much today, a few things from friends. He was due for another trip into the city to flog his professional memory. He needed to keep a sharp balance intact; he felt a horror at losing touch with the unnatural cycle of the city and becoming provincially useless to the business there.

The last time James was in the city, he walked around downtown where he used to reside; very downtown, about as far as you can go. Entering a burrito place across the street from his favorite market he was confronted by a huge poster for some musical performance featuring the former star of a television show. His appetite thus revolted he had turned away and reeled out onto the old familiar sidewalk. In the city things had become healthier, more orderly and fertile for some people. James couldn't be sure if he believed the neighborhood had experienced a conversion or a kind of euthanasia. Long ago, in that same block he'd had his pants front unzipped and inspected by the police. They found no drugs that day, but James had asked the cops, "what do you think?" He assumed they were experts on size and shape.

The last time James was in the city the police seemed happier. Maybe it was a respite. James had to admit he didn't mourn the days of walking out of his door to catch a glimpse of a pregnant drunk bent over, shoving something under her skirt to hide it from a man approaching her with a hammer raised high in the fading glow of the winter sun. That scene must be happening somewhere, still.

James' crazy wife called just after he got home from the post office. She had set out on a drinking and spending binge in Dallas. He kept trying to put off the date of her return, when it was his turn to do so. Before she hung up she said, "I love you."

He sat down and thought of how he had asked the post mistress about the smoke on the ridge and the red sun. He had shown far too much innocence. She squared herself around, firmly planted her feet and squinted at him, "The mountains are burning."

"Oh, I thought maybe they were clearing out the brush before they put in the new cellular towers." He nodded.

This overreach backed her off a little, "No, it's just a wildfire; happens every year."

The land around James' house itself was overgrown. He kept it wild, let the vines crawl where they may. He had thrown down a type of grass seed that grows only five inches high so he wouldn't need to mow it. From the mountain behind the house the flora cascaded seamlessly down into the yard where he had planted flowering vines here and there, azalea bushes, lilies.

His neighbors took a different approach to landscaping. They had hacked a flat and sculpted living space from the shaggy foothills. James could see the far side of the mountain range through their yard, it was like looking from one island to another across a shallow and icy strait pocked with ceramic roosters. They had lived here longer than he had and he felt that their perspective outweighed his own, newer view. A remedy: one wrought-iron fence that would define the shape of his unwelcome landscape and its malign accession to impending ruin.

James had known it was up to him to make the first move, the first concession. Out here people were not direct. They liked to think it civility but James could sense the aggression building. The customary wave the neighbor returned to him by the mailbox every day grew feebler and began to resemble its opposite: the gesture of brushing away. Last week, he had sent out a letter:

Dear Neighbor,

During the year I have lived here I have been attempting to preserve the wild character of the mountains that loom behind my house and even extend the wild design through the whole of my property. Since I have rows of tall trees bordering one of the two exposed sides of my land I had hoped this plan would not ruin the appeal of our shared boundary.

And yet, I felt remorse as the seasons progressed, in winter when the vines withered, the trees dropped and the window of your breakfast area must have served up to you the full effect of this natural work. I recognize that this vista must seem like an act of effrontery on my part, violating as it does the traditions along our shared road.

To correct any awkwardness, I have a proposition that I hope you will find acceptable. I intend (fully at my expense) to erect a fence that would run along the border of our properties. This fence would be of the finest quality black wrought-iron. It would have a rough surface and a half-twist to each post. Each post would stand 4–5 inches from the next and the tops of the posts would terminate in spheres rather than spikes. It would be a stark yet permeable barrier, both pleasing and effective. I feel that in this way I would be respecting your preferred methods of husbandry, drawing an edge to the fine lawn you tend so heartily. Presumably, my vines would begin to entangle with the fence and we would both enjoy the presence of this floral division. Please respond to me at your leisure. I will not proceed with this plan unless and until I have your blessing.

Sincerely Yours,
James Clare

The sun was coming closer to the mountains now and regaining its pale yellow bearing. The fires had carried the dead brush off as intended and the gray sky of a probable snow would soon press in and set the stage for springtime erosion. James backed away from the window and gave a thanks to The Maker, as he imagined was the custom. When he sat down again, he noticed a letter he had missed. It was a response from his neighbor. James read the letter; mortified by its words, he threw it aside. A rush of passion lifted him. He knew where his thoughts would go. He paced the bottom floor, and when that proved insufficient he paced up and down the three flights of stairs.

James had built himself by exploiting a certain formula whereby a person amasses material and social weight in exchange for a share of culpability in the mechanism which supported it, the equivalent of a ransom. Some people settled early, within their family; James searched for wider obligations and tributes, and he had negotiated a settlement with this foreign landscape: a marriage filled by spaces, access to institutions, money free to spend. James believed he could unravel himself from the contract at a time of his choosing. His great triumph had been to have the ransom weighed against a lazy lie, a false name. The letter made him realize it had now swallowed him.

The established precedent, and what one expects to follow a ruin of a mockery of a marriage, would be simply to pass into that free state beyond youthful initiation when all formerly respected institutions are revealed to have been a set of obstacles to which respect must be paid but by which no respect is deserved. After passing through this social awakening any authentic grief could be comforted by the luxury of staging initiations for the next generation of fools willing to accept the same bitter challenges. James had recognized that his wife's recurrent illicit behavior was an overture, an invitation to the mature phase of marriage she had been taught to expect, wherein the partners adventure separately but return to one another, to the homestead, and consolidate their knowledge with new fragments of experience gained among the unwise. James might have reaped forever in contented response to his wife's reckless indulgence. The family and the functions would hold together the necessities and prevent damage to the homeland, drastic cosmetic corrections could be made to keep things upright. James' life could remain safely full of pleasure, it would be like floating down a warm salt waterfall.

But James also knew there would remain many secret spheres he could never penetrate where verdicts were communicated through senses he did not possess. He had some rare talents: honesty, cunning, fear, intimidation, tenderness, vulnerability, sleep. James had resolved to vindicate these skills and not let resentment, suspicion or frustration lead him into privileged liberties or sadism; for example, the serial deflowering of virgins. James could respect the potential for creating such profound and lingering melancholy, he could appreciate the glorious penance paid for pricking in the girl, now a wife, such selfish longings to cause her to retract from the kind gaze of her husband, he could calculate the value derived as the girl recalled to herself a patched fantasy of bliss upon realizing completely she had lost her virginity to the most powerful man she would ever encounter. To combat the obliging lure of this form of relaxation James had been practicing more nuanced and statistical forms of intervention.

Several months back, he had taken to courting internet romances with hurt and beaten women around the country. Women without boundaries in their lives, women bounded entirely by a lack of self-esteem and mobility, women who flirted clumsily in writing, mortifyingly in the flesh, women with no physical self-respect; women young and old used at every turn who persistently threw their needs and lives onto the public phones in pursuit of a cure for their confusion, for a few lines of salacious script or a picture of a hairy, masked man crouching on a bed, masturbating onto a set of *Star Wars* bed sheets. James had wanted to be their angel, to be nice, to be supportive of their crooked dreams. The internet afforded him this chance to do right. He avoided making promises. He would show interest in their worlds and their hurts but he never met them. To discontinue the correspondence had not been difficult because the women tired of the sweetness after a while and gradually stopped responding or else claimed to have met another with whom they had developed a physical relationship. There had been other endeavors, small and practical investigations; and yet, they were played against an undercurrent of fever. The sensible procedure in James' situation was clear and his present isolation now seemed to have been invoked, set aside to him in order that he might grasp the logical conclusions as if they were his own.

James walked to the window and looked down the driveway to the neighbors' house. He remembered in the city he had stood for hours awed in front of a large window that revealed the inner workings of a health club. The runners were trying to extend their lives with vital physical activity; some were drearily wasting lives genetically doomed to early forfeiture by the weakness of their hearts. Not one would admit they'd be better off throwing themselves down on a chair with a box of fried cheese, to more speedily rot by consumption, to do as they were fated. They would not hesitate to tell you what your clothes meant or what your shoes sounded like. They were proud to pay their bills, proud to call the winner a hero, proud to build houses on a foundation of skulls, proud to cry before an execution. James admired their ambitions, never doubted their resolve but was astonished that they stubbornly anticipated some reward beyond the enfranchising complicity so generously granted to them. James had achieved such rewards as they hoped to earn yet they would never accept his authority if he were to suggest they abandon efforts to earn gravity or transcendence and simply create some graceful means to take it, if only to momentarily and rapidly gain an understanding of their limitations. James would be thought a failure with nothing of value to offer them.

This memory raised more frustration but James tried to make of it an inspiration against the possibility of ever accepting the full value of his ransom. His view down the driveway had dimmed somewhat, the hot gasps engendered by his panic fogged the cold winter window he now noticed he had bowed his head against. James slid his fingers across the wet haze and revealed a shard of his neck in reflection. He turned to a bookshelf and searched the spines there for *La Historia de la Vida y Hechos del Emperador Carlos V.* He remembered inside it was a testament from one P. de Sandoval describing the antics of The Flying Witch of Navarre, "slid half-way down a tower like a lizard, flew into the air in sight of all." This was a rare volume, a book not many had seen. This book had never been smuggled by heroic anti-communists or slammed down on a pew in a Gotham church by a blind widow who lost her footing as she knelt to pray. No one had died for this book, apart from the unfortunate peasants who were flayed to make its soft inner bindings; nevertheless, James respected it as surely as he respected the tale of the crucifixion. In an earlier time of life, James had brazenly researched ancient lizard transformations, levitations and other assorted occult human potential. He had discovered that the credible official reports seemed to cease by the eighteenth century. By that point, he had surmised, a limited swath of humanity sublimated these abilities and excluded themselves by preventing the transmission of their genes to those outside of their own kind. This discovery had given him the same vertiginous feeling he got while driving late at night, towards the end of a long drive, when he would begin to reckon that the letters of the green highway signs were arranged in a peculiar fashion. A distinct feeling of inferiority would overwhelm him. If he'd possessed the requisite senses he might have been seeing all manner of announcements or descriptions of events in places to which he remained ignorant and to which he was not invited.

The fever and that vertigo surrounded him now. He had made a mistake. The attempt to connect with his neighbor had seemed like a bold stroke; to solidly bond himself to the countryside and control the house would provide great leverage when the time came to burn it all down along with his wife and her plans for him. James had read the neighbors' reply now and had confronted the final and not oblique failure of an incriminating action. The response verified that James had been replaced by the person he had been imitating all this time, the name by which he had been concealing himself. James read again his own letter. It shocked him. It had been written by that person, his neighbor had been right to be offended at this insultingly condescending interloper, the letter had given just cause for spite. This sudden honesty calmed him and James arrived at the question. He had to sever himself from this life immediately. He would never find the strength, never procure the means to convert it to his will. The system had been working for centuries and although he had taken from it all it could avail him he would never be able to safely dissect it, never alter its purpose. The thought of his wife's smug infallibility goaded him and the neighbors' house sat at the end of his driveway coaxing him like a delicate porcelain fairy stroking her minute, supernatural, unattainable cunt with a taunting sparkle in her eyes.

The deputy had arrested James in the living room of the neighbors' house. James was grinding flowers and pieces of a shattered vase into the carpet with his boot at the time he was apprehended. Earlier, he had stolen through the backdoor and discovered no one at home. Starting on the top floor James had defiled every room, using human fluids or suggestive action obscenities rendered in gray masonry paint. He had tossed all the drawers and closets thoroughly yet stole nothing. He found a lawn mower in the garage and had circled the house with it to destroy the precious gardening. James had then attempted to carve a final obscenity into the deep green grass; meticulous, he had made an effort to orient the words to be read from the house rather then from the street. The excessive gear shifting and the tight turns which had been required of the lawn mower wrenched forth horrible noises and smoke. Before he had been able to trim the full expression from the lawn the engine had seized. Frustrated, James had reentered the house and attacked the living room for a second time. The noise from the lawnmower had been rated suspicious by someone living along the road. They had called the local police.

James rested on a bench across from the deputy as the incident report was being typed up. "You must be shit-faced wasted, Jim," the deputy said. He knew who James was, it was an official familiarity that had afforded James the honor of not being handcuffed. James had gone along willingly to be detained.

"Not at all. That's my wife's department," James said.

"We might need to give a breath test. That's the strangest burglary I've seen. What did they ever do to you?"

"It wasn't a burglary. I went home to the wrong house."

"When I see you around lately you're by yourself. How is your wife?" The deputy asked.

"She's been gone for a few months."

"Problems with the woman? I can believe it, that chick seems pretty wild."

"Not to get personal or shock you but I have to admit that I don't like oral sex. It's a totally bankrupt, intrusive rite. I think I stand almost alone on that side of the issue."

"Is that the problem with her?"

"When I told her about it she was surprised. I think she believed me to be joking. I don't want to force some woman's face down between my legs. It's disrespectful. Isn't it what men like to do to each other, like in prison. You'd know more about that than I."

"Not firsthand. I've always worked out here. I have heard about those things from other officers, though."

"And calling someone a cocksucker is among the most egregious insults one might inflict," James continued.

"But we boys have a gift: jerking off. No woman, no problem," said the deputy.

"I don't like masturbation, either. I got bored with it before puberty was half over. In fact, I get a thrill out of not doing it. I watch pornographic movies just to defile the sacred economy; I can watch them all day and not move a muscle. I can get with real women; but I'm supposedly married. I can't sleep with my wife, I'm more afraid of getting her pregnant than I am of getting AIDS or herpes from her, anymore. Knowing her, she'd be so high while she was carrying that it would get too late to do anything about it and she'd have the baby by accident. That's what I fear most; it's unreasonable but I despise the act of childbirth, it's the only sex I can't watch."

"Sounds like your wife is giving you all sorts of headaches. Is this your first marriage?"

"No," James replied. "It's my third marriage."

"I've seen women that have made men do some much stranger things. I can't blame you for feeling the way that you do. I hope we can work something out about the damage you did to the house. I'll talk with them," the deputy said.

"My wife didn't drive me to do this."

"Well, she didn't help any."

"You got me there," James said.

"This isn't the worst I've ever seen. There was the Miller family, five years ago. Ben Miller killed his father, stabbed him to death. We did our blood work on everyone involved and sent it out to the lab. When it comes back we find that Ben Miller is a hemophiliac but the mother is not." The deputy slammed his palm down on the desk and grinned.

"What does that mean?" James asked.

"Hemophilia is only passed by the mother so there was something wrong. It comes to light that the father we thought Ben had killed was really his mother with a dick sewed on and hair on her tits. The mother knew nothing, not even that Ben's '*father*' had been abusing the boy for years. The lawyers loved us for all that; we were just doing our job but we used taxpayers' money to throw a big fat defense right into their laps."

"What's next for me?" James asked.

"You'll have to come to the courthouse later. You're done for tonight, should I give you a ride home?"

"I think I'd like to walk," James said.

"All right, Mister Clare. I guess you want some time alone."

"I want to walk," James said.

Outside, James saw a cruiser with keys in the ignition. He leaned sideways against the windshield and looked around the interior; there was a shotgun inside and some tools. James stared for a long time. It would be dark for a few more hours and James was still wearing his boots and a sturdy coat. He left the parking lot and walked into the woods. He walked east, away from his house, towards the city. He would travel back there on foot and truly feel the distance. He would walk right into the center of town and try to find any friend he could find. He would plead with them to take him in and he would apologize to them for abandoning his place.

2

VAN CAMP'S

Lilly was peeling carrots in the kitchen when Karen walked in and tried to look at the top shelf without Lilly noticing. The last can of Van Camp's Pork and Beans was hidden there behind the flour.

"Do you need something?" Lilly asked.

"I thought I might have left my glasses in here," Karen said.

"Did you check the shower? You've left them in there before. You always take so long in there."

"I have a certain routine I have to follow. It takes me five minutes just to wash between my toes, for example."

"You stand on one leg to wash each foot? That's dangerous," Lilly warned.

"I'm very careful. How else can I get my feet clean? I hate taking baths," Karen explained.

"I just let my feet get clean as I go along. It saves on water. You should try being a little less particular, less selfish. We're four in this house now. Where do you think all that dirty water goes?"

"You don't even recycle. You're wasting your time trying to get me to feel bad about my showers," Karen said.

"I'm sorry. I want everyone in this house to feel comfortable. I thought I might mention it since you are the strongest one. Besides, I do recycle. I keep all our plastic bags under the sink. Look around the house, I put a lot of old trash to use. I don't just toss it out. How about that hurricane lantern I made for you out of the pork and beans can? You find that useful. Now you can read your magazines all night without keeping me up," Lilly said.

Chuck came into the kitchen. He had been sitting on the edge of the bathtub with the door locked. When he heard the women talking he buttoned up his pants and left the washroom to join them.

"Have you seen my glasses, Chuck?" Karen asked.

"They weren't in the washroom," Chuck said.

Lilly raised her eyebrows. "Were you in the bathroom? How long were you in there?"

"Do you want to know if it was a number two?" Chuck asked, irritated.

"You know what I mean," Lilly said. "We have to keep to the schedule. There are too many people in this house, now."

"I was starting to use the facilities but then I realized what time it was. I can wait."

"You go ahead, Chuck. I wanted to make you aware of it. We were just discussing how difficult this adjustment will be for us," Lilly said.

"It's better if I get used to sticking with the schedule. I'd rather talk with you two. Are we doing anything tonight?" Chuck asked.

Karen moved to the back wall and stood before the shelves. "When Mack finishes his last delivery we can eat dinner," she said.

"And then what?" Chuck asked.

Lilly spoke sharply: "There's no need to be sarcastic. We don't have to plan out each and every minute. I said that you could go use the bathroom. Just hurry, before Mack gets home."

"I'm not joking. I was hoping we could do something tonight," Chuck said.

"I could call Will," Karen said. She turned to Lilly to see if it was all right. Lilly didn't seem to disapprove of the suggestion. She did seem to be looking past Karen to the top shelf. Karen moved away from the shelves, feigning indifference.

"If Chuck doesn't mind—the way Will picks on him sometimes makes me very uncomfortable," Lilly said.

"It doesn't bother me," Chuck said.

"Are you feeling sociable today, Chuck?" Lilly asked.

"Since we have to all be here together, I figure why fight to be alone? Will doesn't really bother me. He's tough, I can respect that. We should enjoy the crowd we have. It wasn't very long ago I was stuck in the city next to a billion other people—but as lonely as if I'd been out on the ice somewhere," Chuck said.

The front door opened and Mack entered, returned from his final run of the day. Lilly and Chuck left the kitchen to greet them. Karen grabbed the lone portion of pork and beans from the shelf. She opened the cabinet under the sink and pressed the perfectly cylindrical and gorgeously weighted can deep inside a cardboard box filled with plastic grocery bags. She closed the cabinet softly and then made a show of rummaging through the drawer of forks and spoons on the opposite side of the room.

"I can't find those glasses anywhere," she announced as she left the kitchen to welcome Mack home.

"Have you heard from your wife lately, Mack?" Lilly asked as she served dinner.

"I hear she's the same as always," Mack said.

"I wish you could resolve this. No one else seems to mind but your wife wears on me. It's a swollen spot of unfinished business. I realize you don't have money to pay a lawyer but there must be some measure you can afford to take," Lilly said.

"Let's talk about this later," Mack said.

"You always say you will have time for it on a later day," Lilly said. "You're living here now so you should be able to save some money and take care of this dreadful situation. What else have you to look after? People like us cannot afford too many mistakes; you should take care of this one before you make another. I understand that your wife complains that she has had a difficult time, where she comes from; but you can't fix the life she's had."

"You mean her ex-husband," Karen said.

"The one that put her in the hospital." Chuck added.

"That's enough. I'm only trying to describe my sense that Mack should not have expected to overcome his wife's troubles, to correct her mistakes. Two people, so far removed from each other by what they don't share cannot hope to heal the pain they carry to each other," Lilly said.

"Are you saying it is my fault?" Mack asked.

"Let's agree that not one of us should feel badly when we try to help someone and fail. It might seem like we have a duty to aid lesser people but I don't know who granted us that burden. We try if we have the time but it isn't our foremost mission. As long as any of us can remember we've suffered like the others. Your father once said, when we first took the moon: 'the only thing we can't stand is a complication.' We shook our fists at polio and said: 'the only thing we can't stand is being intimidated by our inferiors.' We simply defend what everyone knows is right. We are only like all the rest. We don't have to set an example," Lilly said.

"The Wildcats' varsity basketball team are playing at the high school tonight. I was going to go," Mack said, changing the subject.

"Will is coming by," Lilly reminded him.

"He's going to the game with me," Mack said.

"Are you all going to the game?" Chuck asked nervously. He could see himself, one hour hence, alone in the house with a feeling of liberation and privacy overwhelming him. Chuck tried to expel the sultry images emerging, the acts he longed to witness and immerse himself within. He began transposing the encroaching procession of delights with certain pictures from violent news items he remembered seeing earlier that afternoon. "It's happening again isn't it," he thought. "Is this magic? Those refugees attacked in their camp—were they wanderers or immigrants? The bodies from that series of final offenses, obese self-sacrifice cannonball divers." The fireworks show distracted him temporarily but in spite of the vegetative effects of these horrors warmly gratifying urges stole through his head.

"How about the game, Lilly?" Karen suggested.

"I think I'd like to go to the game," Lilly said.

"Then don't hang around here when Will comes, you should just make it on time," Karen said.

"You don't seem to have much of an appetite," Lilly replied.

"I've been trying to eat bigger breakfasts. I was getting tired at work."

"If you get hungry before bed there's probably a snack in the kitchen."

"I don't like to eat too much at night. I wake up tired if I do that."

"Don't be silly, if you are hungry you should eat."

"I don't think there's anything left on the shelves, Lilly. It's almost time to do the shopping."

"I thought there were a few cans of something. I can check for you. That reminds me, I need to get those bags out from under the sink. They pay two cents for each at Costwell. Combine that with the coupons and we save a good amount. I've really had to declare war on the shopping since there are so many of us now," Lilly said.

"I'll get those bags out when I do the dishes," Karen said.

"I think Mack's name is on the chore board."

"We're trading spots."

"That's sweet. Mack worked hard all day and he deserves a little relaxation," Lilly said.

"How was dinner?" Will asked as he stood near the front door. He didn't remove his coat.

"Dinner was good," Mack said. "Come in and sit down. We don't need to leave yet."

"If it's all right with you, Karen, I'd like to come in," Will said.

"Why should it matter to me?" Karen asked.

"It's not that it would matter to you if I stayed, I was just making sure it wouldn't interfere with social plans that anyone might have had for this evening," Will said.

"I'm going to the basketball game. It was Karen's idea," Lilly said to Will.

"That sounds fun. Is Karen going?" Will asked.

"You didn't say you were going, Karen," Chuck moaned.

"Why aren't you going, Chuck?" Will asked. "Do you have some videos to watch? We could all stay here and watch them with you, unless they're the kind you watch alone."

Karen interrupted before Chuck had a chance to get angry, "I'm staying here. Will, Mack and Lilly are going to the game."

"What about the videos?" Will asked.

Mack broke in, "Forget that, we're all going to go see the Wildcats."

"Why don't you go to the game with us, Karen?" Will asked.

"She just said she's staying here," Mack pointed out.

"I have chores to do," Karen said.

"I can give you a hand in the kitchen," Chuck said.

"After you give yourself a hand in the bathroom," Will said. He laughed at his own joke, expecting the others to join in.

Mack drew Will into the kitchen by offering him something to drink. "Will, you take Lilly to the game in your car. I'll meet you there later," Mack said. "I have to go see my wife. I promised Karen. She's been worried about her. Don't bring it up, though, Karen doesn't want Lilly to know. I'll say I had to run back by the depot or something."

"I got it," Will said as he opened the refrigerator door, searching for a beer. "Karen looks nice without her glasses. Did she get contact lenses?"

"What are you doing? I brought you in here to talk. We have to get moving," Mack said.

Karen had become nervous for her can of pork and beans when she saw the pair enter the kitchen. She watched their hands and pockets closely as they came back into the living room. She had saved her appetite at dinner and the hunger was making her anxious. Will noticed her gaze and took the opportunity to compliment Karen on her new contact lenses.

"I lost my glasses," Karen explained.

"It's still a good look for you," Will said. "Unless it hurts your eyes. Where did you lose your glasses?"

"I don't know. I looked all over the house. You better get going. You should go to the game, Chuck," Karen said.

Lilly had been patient but these circular and disorderly negotiations were intolerable. She had hoped they would reach some balance by their own efforts but it was getting late. "We've already established who is staying and going, Karen. I've never witnessed a more senseless waste of time. We have entirely agreed upon every detail yet as we stand three feet from the door, on the very threshold of stepping outside, we have suddenly become confused and timid. No one is applying the tenacity needed to make this living arrangement work. Just let's everyone go do what we all had planned to do and everyone have a good time."

As Lilly donned her jacket, Karen was filled with anticipation. A taste of the pungent pork and beans stood but one more obstacle distant. Karen thought she could hear the sleek can of pork and beans rustling itself inside the nest of plastic bags, slinking from its colorful wrapper, rolling towards her, submissive and intent. Karen touched her face. She was blushing.

"We're off to the game," Will said to Karen, boldly. He had mistaken Karen's color for a demur flirtation. "If you're awake when we get back I can help you look for your glasses."

"Have a good time," Karen said, not at all hearing Will.

Once she had dismissed her rivals Karen shouted: "Finally!"

"I didn't want them to leave," Chuck said.

"You had every chance to go. Lilly was right to say we have to work harder at living together. I'll do my part tonight," Karen said.

"I am glad you stayed," Chuck said.

"You aren't hungry are you?"

"Not at all."

"Good, then here's what's going to happen: I'm going into the kitchen, you can come with me. I'm going to cook myself a snack. We will sit here on the couch together until the others return," Karen explained.

"What about looking for your glasses?" Chuck asked.

"Let's not do that. We shouldn't go off separately. I want to sit here on the couch and partake of the pork and beans I have been waiting to eat. I'm going to help you. You must sit here with me until they return. All I ask is that you do not speak to me while I am eating, you do not dare to ask me for a taste of pork and beans, you do not express any displeasure at the predictable disturbances which will occur once I have consumed the pork and beans. Do we have a deal, Chuck?"

"It is a fair price to pay to have you stay here with me. I'll sit here and watch you eat," Chuck said.

3

PATIENCE
(WITH COMMENTARY)

"Carelessness keeps people from thinking
about the renewal of their lives."
John Calvin

I was asked by the editor of this magazine to report about "whatever is
coming across the scanner." Being country, as I am, I immediately recognized a phrase of jargon. After some thought, I parsed the request
to mean "generalized observations from the wilderness."

Out here in the wilderness there is a shopping mall. A few weeks
ago I found myself in one of its stores. This was a store for teen fashion
and, therefore, music videos were playing on TV screens mounted on
its mirrored walls. Behind me, I could hear a young girl masticating
along with the song. During the rhythm break she turned to her com-
panion and, referring to the image on the screen, said cheerily, "Look,
his dog is just like my dog." I turned around and asked, "Is that what
they're calling a fat ass these days—'my dog' ?"

I wasn't there to buy anything and yet I had been given a gift: a new
term in slang. In this time when we have such a vast array of stimulus
available: a stadium concert where a polysexual demon is nailed to a
cross, any image the mind can desire accessed with the mere click of
a button, the ability to travel anywhere on Earth at anytime at a low
price, professional basketball played completely nude; in these days,
still it persists: the banal can be made profound once again through
the rejuvenation of language.

I always take heed of the passionately amnesiac, like the voices that
scream for change in the wake of these many shootings in our schools

across America, "Save the children from these wretched devils—the precious children." Even though I know it is the same old bloodshed, even though I recall the gunman who burst into my high school back in the eighties and took the principal hostage, even though I remember the kid who hung himself in a tree in his front yard so that his ex-girlfriend would see him there on her way to school; despite all of my memories, I respect the feelings that parents have that there has never been a more valuable soul than their own child and that these times (now) are the most difficult the world has ever faced. The replication of one's DNA, the most basic of animal drives, is made sacred and supremely transcendent through the mere, and yet abundantly taxing, rejuvenation of the language.

I despise children individually as I confront them day-to-day yet I find myself swept up in the love for "the children" as a whole. I feel it is true that "every year should be the year of the child." I know that each blessed infant is really just a parasitic weed designed by nature to carry the life-force forward by whatever brutal means required yet I find myself swept up in the reaffirmation of the obvious. I feel impelled to cast my life seed in with the scramble because I believe once again.

And so, with this in mind, I will turn my face towards the future and make this special announcement: I am offering my seed to any female who wishes to conceive and bear a child. Genetically, my credentials are top-notch and I have copious test results available that detail both my physical and mental qualities. These statistics will be made available to all serious candidates. A legal arrangement will be devised and agreed to whereby my status in the life of the future-child will be defined based on the desires of the mother. I have no wish to burden my progeny with a bizarre past, and yet, I would be more than willing to give limited emotional and financial support, within reasonable guidelines also set forth in a binding legal agreement. Insemination may take place by natural or artificial means, as the mother sees fit.

All interested parties should contact me through the editor of this magazine and my lawyer will then begin the negotiations. Naturally, some screening of candidates will take place but I assure you that I have a wide-ranging affection for the multivariate biological and cultural density of the human race and any objections I might have to an individual would be based on such things as incompatible blood-types or the possibility of genetic mutations that may threaten the life of the future-child.

Patience. The title seems disassociated, it places one marker a full distance away from the main drive of the article in an attempt to center the reader and bring the two ideas close to each other. A title, or headline, is usually printed in bold and is the first, sometimes the only, text on a magazine page to be read; mistitling the article deceives superficial examination.

Report about, "whatever is coming across the scanner." This revelation of the misguided attitude of the editor fixes the author within a commercial framework and simultaneously expresses a bemused perspective. If a man can claim no geographical birthright he should be willing to assume a variety of masquerades as the situation dictates. An advantage may be obtained in absolution from a primal location by forcing antagonists to respond by claiming allegiance to a geographic identity.

The wilderness. In this competitive confrontation, between the urban and the outside, alliance is unnecessary in terms of the relative advantage of one location over another. Viewing landscapes contiguously is preferable since cognitive fragmentation is customary when hierarchal, geographic shorthand is utilized to clarify perspective. It is better to feel comfortable while adapting to a site than to feel compelled to alter a venue by interpretation so it will conform to a fixed perspective. The correct struggle conforms perspective through its application to present cases, while not abandoning all previous observations in order to see clearly. Patience allows curiosity to thrive during the clash of the exotic with the familiar.

Out here in the wilderness there is a shopping mall. This sardonic leveling of the editorial perspective attacks the habit of organizing a chaotic landscape into geometrically pure units and appeals to the curiosity of those who suspect there is not an overwhelmingly final weight of evidence to justify capitulating to the presumption that all good things gravitate in an unerring way toward the center of power. Although anomalies are irritating, we should acknowledge the possibility that resistance can arise which does not need to deny the facts of power. It would be wise to remember this possibility without having to choose between authority or oppression when characterizing the relationship between an individual and the whole. Patience is needed so that the exigencies of opinion do not hasten the imposition of a limited scope of observation. Patience also prevents the adoption of willfully contrary beliefs in the face of seemingly indisputable opinions.

Is that what they're calling a fat ass these days—'my dog'? The author aligns himself with an elitist point of view when casting this insult in order to erect the means by which a flaw of logic undermines the sanctity and authority of that viewpoint. The action of making that caustic remark demonstrates a mechanism whereby impatience sows the seed of negation within the distance separating and differentiating the two individuals involved.

In these days, still it persists: the banal can be made profound once again through the rejuvenation of language. Information is satisfying. The use of harmless language to reinvent the interest of a thing generates new information while reaffirming the exertion of language without the incriminating responsibility of denotation. Patience, in this regard, affords one the selective examination of a variety of perspectives beyond the indemnifying reservations of exclusive and consistent language. Singular or specialized demands, rituals of graduated servitude and unassailability must compete with the rejuvenation of language and not merely cultivate or oppose the secret bitterness of the excluded or servile.

The passionately amnesiac. This phrase is meant to identify a trait which can be superceded in ourselves and others by patient examination and rejuvenation. Many times, when confronting some obstacle a dissolution of experience transpires in the belief that passion might elevate the expression of an irrationally fixed doctrine.

Replication . . . made sacred . . . through . . . rejuvenation of the language. Genetic passions and the biologically absolute can disrupt the process of rejuvenation within the bounds of conflict if the foundation from which proceeds the competitive relationship requires the reinvention of the primacy of biology. Citizenry is a human creation which allows for fiction, ignorance or stability to disrupt or guide the course of things without respect for absolutes. Patience is crucial to recognizing the separation of the truly unchanging and the chaotic creations of humankind.

A parasitic weed. The author presents a condescending view of the biological drives which seem central to the political lives of many human beings. This attitude assists in erecting a structure to be dismantled by an unprompted and unfounded accession to human nature. Lurking behind the distaste, detachment silently erodes patience. The imminent collapse will be caused by an internalized, fixed notion of organization which does not allow for the shifts of human will which underlie and can alter any logic, principle or assumption.

I am offering my seed to any female who wishes to conceive and bear a child. After attempting to dictate and define the relationship the author bears towards this "wilderness" presumably beyond the sphere of the magazine reader, total surrender occurs. It might be presumed to illustrate the ease with which an individual can cross cultural barriers when that individual feels superior to the concerns of those who passionately believe in the absolute truth of any boundary intended to define identity. In actuality, it reveals the desperation of the author, ineffectually masked by stiff and pompous satirical language. The spiritual challenge invoked by this epistle is whether we can conduct the sources of patience beyond falling prey to random assertions or patterns offered as truth. Orchestrated dissent disallows confrontations which lead to transformation; conversely, patience in the guise of detachment creates an abyss of dislocation and allows various persuasive forces to generate a weight of evidence to maintain distinct classifications which convert chaotic human life into predetermined relationships while suspending patience to the point of alienation.

4

BACK TO THE NOWHERE

Ignorance mingled with memories; Maynard struggled the length of a funeral service to remember why there had to be a rail around the coffin. He was certain it was attached, a spacer that guided the body down the grave wall. Maynard accompanied the widow to her car. She was a lifelong friend to him now bereaved, without a husband.

"What a waste of money for this," she said.

Maynard comforted her but only as a stranger would do; he wanted to talk to her like a friend, dismiss his responsibilities and make a joke about the way the minister had mispronounced her husband's middle name. To the contrary, he was rock solid.

The widow, Jackie Harris, could not engage his kindness. She was preoccupied by the tasks awaiting her among the living. Determined to overwhelm every account of survivorship, she had invested no energy in public mourning. She had a lot of financial and legal steps to fulfill and she wanted to attack them. She felt like she wanted to talk to Maynard as a friend, the way they had talked to each other in the past, at another time of possibility. Whenever she interrupted his passive applications he showed pity as if she were trying to conceal her sorrow. There was no sorrow in her but that the conversation was misguided. Jackie tried one last time to show Maynard how she was feeling, Maynard tried to interject with some levity. They shook hands.

From the warm expanse of a laughing face to the perpetually ailing aunt who needed a ride home, Maynard attended to what was before him; he was a good friend, like a politician, although he never made bargains for his services; just to be one to whom people could turn was honor enough. He had two jobs, in a way, including a clock job at the Motor Vehicle Department. Here at The Maryland House it was warm and everyone was getting drunk. Maynard was the lifeguard. It had been so since he had abandoned his youthful musical endeavors, a project his kindness had helped to degrade. There was an unsatisfying competition in the performing arts. One had to study and work very hard and yet the final determinations were made by luck. It was a craft to create a human response in performance yet real status came from the craft of inhuman calculation.

One night at The Maryland House, back when his musical skills were admired, before Jackie had given up music and married, Maynard walked off the stage and was appalled at how his public display had queered the behavior of the same people who had treated him in a rough, familiar way but an hour before. The craft involved failing to notice that effect. It was crucial to understand the inspiration behind it and respect the rights of every person to lose themselves in a little dream. Maynard had failed because of both his kindness and his contempt. The musical group broke up soon after that night and the singer moved to a bigger city to pursue success. Maynard had stayed in town and loved people better by avoiding that strange relationship which caused him such pain.

Jackie strolled around boxes and piles of clothes down on the first floor of the house that belonged to her now, free and clear. She had been living down on the first floor since last year, avoiding her husband. She started singing and dancing to the music on the stereo, her toes gliding past stacks of bank receipts and cancelled checks. Later, she shredded them and tossed them into the dumpster by the back alley along with four garbage bags filled with mens' clothing.

She mixed some whiskey into her coffee and sipped it while going through a notebook of lists and deadlines. Nearly all were complete. She had been attesting and attending to each required vow and sub-jecting herself to examination by those who wished to confirm her as the dutiful wife of a dead man. They could not sense her excitement as each successive obligation was met. Every step severed another bond to the guilt she had assumed by indenturing herself to his family. Despite the complexity of the law, marriage was still blindly esteemed; Jackie herself held it in high regard in the sense that it had been the most challenging labyrinth to which she could have confined herself.

She rolled back the top of a piano keyboard. The small piano had been carted into this spot after her wedding. It had been a piece of dead furniture in the room since that day, a chunk of wood convenient to hold mail or stacks of magazines. The piano hadn't caused Jackie any remorse, it was a sturdy machine waiting and hiding alongside her until the false character of the connubial house transformed from what Jackie knew to be merely a temporary state of siege.

Jackie spread her fingers out and played two major chords. She listened with affection to the dry and sour tone of each mallet striking. Jackie tried to find a note to sing that could please the sounds and bring them closer. She played the chords and let them ring, the sounds arranged themselves around her and pushed her voice. The tempo and tones elevated her and the neglected instruments, her voice and the piano, extended together to fill the room.

Maynard went to The Maryland House during his lunch break. Every noon he would hear what news there was and tell what he had heard. Someone's daughter broke her hip last night and Maynard volunteered to bring some cheeseburgers to her house. While he waited for the order he took a beer for himself and talked with some friends, anyone who happened to be there.

The door opened while he was talking about car insurance, a man walked inside but Maynard didn't recognize him since the sun was behind the man. The door closed in precise timing with the stride of the man towards Maynard. There was a sound from the door snapping shut and then a voice: "First place I think of looking for you, I find you."

Maynard was outraged by the dramatic entrance; although unlikely it had been planned, the man who spoke those words had always seemed to have good luck. He involved and attracted the space around him without seeming to notice or to care.

"I'm back, comrade." The man spoke again.

Maynard was embarrassed by the endearment. It came from a time when musical groups adopted solidarity with the proverbial working by such superficial means as peasant caps or dyed hair. It had been

eemed so from the magazines, back when Maynard
h Cliff. They had absorbed as many ideas as they
ey wanted to be vital. They had performed songs
............y political concerns. Maynard cringed as the music
sputtered through his memory like a faulting bottle rocket. He could
see the shoddy musical instruments they had played: battery powered
drums, cracked plastic keys, bright pink guitars. It angered him and
he could not speak.

"I should have called but you'll forgive me because I have big news
for you," Cliff said as he sat down at the bar.

"I guessed you might come back to see Jackie," Maynard said.

"Her too, sure; this is big for all of us."

"I thought that you'd come for the funeral."

"Not unless you mean the scene inside this place." Cliff smiled.

"Jackie's husband died," Maynard said.

"That's too bad. To be honest I never really liked him." Cliff leaned
over the bar and grabbed a handful of olives.

"Don't you want to know how she's doing?" Maynard asked.

"Let's take a drive, pick her up and go somewhere nice where we can
talk. I can cheer you all up. I want to get the band back together." Cliff
slipped an olive pit out of his mouth.

"I don't care what you want. I do care about Jackie because she needs
my help and she's my friend. All of my other friends and all the people
who used to like you, too, are still here and that's where a friend has got
to be to be a friend. Talk all you want or take a fucking drive, I have to
get back." Maynard grabbed the sack of cheeseburgers and departed.

Seeing Cliff again had put a stain on the day, one delay led to
another and a backed up line at work led to a late arrival at Jackie's
house. When cars passed the wooden steps waiting could be inter-
posed with rehearsals of apology; with each car Maynard refined a
greeting for Jackie. He worried he might start overbearingly, his sym-
pathy composed of motivational tones. If this alteration in Jackie's life
could change him it would be the proper time to tell her how he was
feeling. If he saw the right signs he would follow them. A car passed,
he looked up and saw Cliff.

"I took a walk," Cliff said. "I wanted to come see Jackie but I find you here instead." Cliff patted Maynard's shoulder and sat down next to him.

"She isn't home," Maynard said.

"We can talk until she returns. Maybe we'll be happy by the time she gets here. She might like that better than the way it was at the bar."

"She'll be glad to see you, glad to see us together," Maynard admitted.

"I'm sorry I pissed you off. I was talking big because I was nervous. I'd hoped you'd be excited to see me."

"Tell me the story. Why have you come back?"

"I don't want to go into everything until we can work things out. Even then, I might not tell you the truth," Cliff said.

"I recall so many times you saved me trouble in that way; holding back details you thought might scare or disturb me," Maynard said.

"I always looked up to you," Cliff said.

"You'd have to get down on the floor to look up to me now." Maynard meant to say he wasn't feeling bitter.

"Even though you knew the band was a joke, you always took music seriously and pushed us to get better."

"I didn't want us to be killing ourselves for nothing. Friendship and self-respect are valuable, too."

"So what is your excuse now?" Cliff asked.

"Even though you have a lot you can hold over my head, know that I take my life for fact." Maynard pointed a finger at Cliff's right eye.

"I haven't changed, either," Cliff said.

"There's no weight here for you to throw around," Maynard said.

"It's a habit."

"I remember."

"Let's go. She's probably busy with all that death bullshit," Cliff said.

"Let's go get a drink. I'll come by here tomorrow. I'd like to find out why you had to come crawling back here."

"I'm sure you'll get a kick out of my dismal failure."

"I'll leave a note and tell Jackie that I saw you." Maynard walked up the porch steps.

"Will you and she finally get together?" Cliff asked.

"You've been gone from this place a long time," Maynard said. "We don't have happy endings here."

The note was still wedged into the screen door when Maynard came by Jackie's house the next day. He suspected she was climbing in and out of the house by the back stairs. Jackie looked tired when she answered the door. Maynard bristled when he saw her face. He pushed his way inside.

"Does everything have to be a war with you? I got some forms from the city clerk. Go get all the papers out and I'll help you take care of this—unless you're sick or something."

"I'm on top of it," Jackie said.

"Don't make this difficult. You go through what you need to go through; I'm just trying to help you. Now that your situation has upended, I'm sure you're worried what your life will be like. I can help you get organized, go get the papers." Maynard waved his hand towards the front room.

"You're too late to help me with my life. You sat and watched while it was ruined. You're going into your nurse routine now but you let me go through hell for years. You don't know what it's been like for me," Jackie said.

"I respected the choices you made, Jackie. That's what I thought a friend should do. If you had reached out to me I would have responded. It didn't seem right to interfere. When you love someone I think you give them room to make their own choices. You're strong. I figured you were in control."

"You really don't know how I was living?" Jackie asked. She watched Maynard's face carefully.

"It was off limits," Maynard said.

"You gave up music just to stay in town and watch me suffer."

"I've been thinking that about myself. I did give it up for you. I loved you."

"I want to keep this time to myself," Jackie said. "I can't think past that."

"I wanted to be honest. I've been thinking about it since I saw Cliff," Maynard said.

"When did you see Cliff?" Jackie asked.

"I should have said something. When I saw you I got mad. I left a note. Did you get it?"

"I've been busy taking care of everything, like I said. Do you think I'm lying?"

"I'm just feeling a little raw," Maynard admitted.

"Just forget about all this. We have plenty of time to talk. Let's go see Cliff. Let's just forget all this shit—it isn't us. We used to have fun."

"I can't remember." Maynard looked around the room. The clutter had been thinned out considerably. The piano was open. There were boxes stacked neatly by the back door. He walked to a set of bookshelves and ran his fingers along a row of old vinyl record albums.

"I pulled my stuff back out," Jackie said. "This place is all mine now. I've been listening to music again. By tomorrow, there won't be one trace of him left in this house."

"You saved all these. I threw mine out," Maynard said.

The sweet amber swirled across the teeth and grease filtered light cast dim guided eyes across pool tables ranged in procession towards the dark of the washroom stalls. Jackie held the nearest table for seven games and the boys watched her.

"She has changed," Cliff said.

"In the past week," Maynard said.

Cliff had explained why he had returned to them. The explanation had been prosaic for Jackie's benefit as he wished to bring himself down into their lives without making Maynard seem dull. He had been scheming how to best pull them both into his plans.

"I think playing music again will help both of you. You will get to see each other as much as ever but you'll both be in your finest element," Cliff said.

"It seemed like you had made such a big name for yourself. It's awkward for me to imagine playing with you. I had consigned you to that other world; I feel like an amateur."

"Just do your job, you were never any good at the business side of it. I'll do all that. I'm not going to pretend you will get a lot of attention, maybe it's better for you that way. I fell pretty low after I had that hit song on the movie soundtrack. I can't get anything done up there, now. With you I can build something off of that success. We'll make great money playing at the casinos."

"I told Jackie that I loved her," Maynard said.

"What did she say?" Cliff asked.

"Nothing," Maynard said.

"That's good. She's busy dancing on his grave. I think if the two of you come in with me you'd be helping her without having to play the father like you used to. There's no room for that shit."

"She's having a good time," Maynard said as he tilted his glass towards Jackie, who was at that moment performing a mock execution with her pool cue on the neck of her latest eight-ball victim.

She rejoined the boys at the bar. Nothing remotely serious intruded on them until closing time. Cliff deviously promoted this reunion of old friends and Jackie carried it to extremes by making Maynard talk about the car he would buy or what kind of big rings he might wear after they cut anchor from this shitty life and went back to the way things used to be. This time they would do it right, Cliff reminded them when he could say it in a pleasantly challenging way. After a while, Jackie was too drunk and had grabbed her pool cue again to use as a guitar. She straddled the jukebox like it was a mechanical bull, one that could pump sound between her thighs as it bucked.

The two men were only half as drunk so Jackie had the advantage of sarcasm. Since she had recently been close to a death they didn't get angry with her as they drove her home, they didn't have any leverage. Cliff joked around with her to keep the camaraderie alive, to simulate the feelings he hoped would eventually lead them both to agree to play in his band.

Maynard experimented with a sullen attitude. He liked the balance between the three of them and that made him feel good about the future. Anything would be better than what had passed between him and Jackie earlier that afternoon. Thinking of it, he felt like he had been speaking captions from greeting cards. That was all he'd had up his sleeve, a big stack of them and the sentiments and wishes they contained circumscribed his life; once it had been popular songs on the radio, before that it had been the things he heard from his parents or the toughest kids in school.

When Cliff and Maynard set Jackie down on her bed she took some final slashes at them. She was profound, perched at the edge of unconsciousness. She wanted to leave them with the hardest part of her and keep them up for while thinking about, to guard her door while she slept.

"Listen, I have worked everything for us and it worked out like we planned. When you go to decide about this, especially you, Maynard, take the money off the table. Cliff won't have to carry us. I have worked it out," Jackie said.

"You have it all planned out?" Cliff smiled.

"Had! It's done now. Here's what happened now and just between us I will tell you. My husband was coming back down the back stairs. To get me, I'm pretty sure. He got home with someone, a girl, and I was getting ready to get out of there and go to Miranda's house. I heard them up there and then she left and a little after he came down to get me and he fell over the rail on the stairs. He knew he wouldn't get through the front door but the kitchen door has a cheap lock so he came down the back stairs and he fell, those stairs are steep. I watched him on the ground for a few minutes and got my sweater on and went to Miranda's. She never heard me come in and so I just went to sleep. So I get the insurance money and the best thing about it is they can't do shit to me. I'm so glad you are both here. I can't believe it. It is going to be fine. Sleep out there and we can get lunch in the morning when we wake up."

Maynard and Cliff were suddenly standing up next to the bed as if she had commanded them to do so; during her confession they had risen from the mattress in a slow, shocked ovation.

"She's knocked out," Cliff said. He gestured for Maynard to follow him into the front room. They sprawled out on a couch and a chair.

"That was how he died, it's true. He fell off the back stairs," Maynard said. "Jackie told the police she was at Miranda's the entire night."

"What the hell happened to this place?" Cliff pinched his forehead. "I remember when we broke into Petty's apartment to get your guitar back that was like the crime of the century."

In the morning, they left before Jackie was awake. They wandered around downtown and into the music store there. Maynard didn't like the way contemporary guitars looked. He had an old guitar, although it had been modern when he bought it.

"It's like a toy store in there," Maynard said. They were standing outside now. Maynard felt awkward, like a loitering pervert.

"It was always that way, we didn't know any better. I can get great deals on equipment. I can get good shit back in the city. Take your hands out of your pockets; I thought you were getting comfortable with playing music again."

"This store makes me depressed. I haven't been inside it for a long time," Maynard said.

"This place is for kids. Music is a good hobby but this place isn't for us. You're an old-timer now," Cliff said. "When I came back here I thought I would dazzle you and make myself feel better. I can see now that you've been holding onto it. I have come to believe we can truly do this and make a good bundle of cash. What do you think?"

"I'd like Jackie to see me in a different light. Maybe you can give me advice on what clothes I should buy," Maynard said.

"I will be doing that," Cliff said. He ran his finger through the air and traced Maynard's attire from toe to top. "I'll have to get everyone hooked up."

5

TRAVEL DIARY

KNOXVILLE, TN—My driver arrived at eight in the morning, just in time for me to go to sleep. That great old Baptist church downtown has been converted into a buffalo wing restaurant. My driver was from England. He's married to an old girlfriend of mine. She was nice but she always made me go out to the courtyard of her apartment to get high.

ATLANTA, GA—Just before beginning today's promotional activities I received word from home that one of my cats had taken ill. I told the radio interview that I lived in Virginia now.

"Whereabouts is that?" He asked.

"Between Maryland and North Carolina," I said.

I was being interviewed by the unfortunately named Wayne Williams. When I attempted to work that into a joke he again was perplexed. To the next question I answered in my impersonation of an athlete's standard phrasing: "We're just going to play our game and stay within ourselves. We're going to concentrate on fundamentals and God willing if we stay healthy we'll come out on top." Nothing. Jimmy told me that all of his friends here are already getting evicted from their apartments in advance of the Olympics (that fascist passion play!) so the landlords can cash in.

NASHVILLE, TN—Patrick said he doesn't like working with women, admits he "has a problem." If the color of your hair is brighter than the color of your Christmas tree . . . you might be from the south. I'm working on some jokes but that syntax might be patented. Here's another: "High school is rough for everyone. In high school I played sports but I liked to read; I was half jock and half nerd so I spent a lot of time beating myself up." Nashville is an entertainment industry center where they need ideas about "money for Velveeta and burial plots" not "super magnets and fucking in hydrogen-powered cars." We drove through Arkansas. There were twenty cars parked at one rest stop, in each car people were sleeping, vulnerable.

SHREVEPORT, LA—The doleful tranquility of yesterday gave way to diabolically restless dreams. Patrick put five eggs in his mouth and Jimmy drank cold pancake batter. Jill confessed that this excursion has helped to actualize her powers. I fight against the psychic intrusion but I cannot sustain; we have capitulated to the decrees of the spirit, and by extension the will of America.

Jimmy sauntered in wearing a full tuxedo. "I'm off the hook," he said.

"That's some funny shit," Jill said.

"I'm laying down the law around here. I'm the new sheriff in town," Jimmy said.

"Are you scared?" Jill asked him.

"I just put a French bread pizza in the microwave oven," he responded.

"I'm rooting for you, Jimmy. I'll even make for you an aluminum foil star," Patrick said.

HOUSTON, TX—I'd like to purchase one of those air cannons that shoot heavy beanbags. They can knock a man flat. I would put glitter in there, too, just for fun.

AUSTIN, TX—After my last meeting for the day I was walking back to the hotel when some redneck in a Nissan jumped the curb. He drove down the sidewalk for a block and swerved through the glass of my hotel's lobby. I watched them clean it up for twenty minutes. A nice looking lady showed up, hysterical; the cops kept her away from the wreck. I heard her say that the driver was her father. They let her ride in the ambulance with the body. The next day, I saw a story about the crash in the newspaper, the driver had died. They had printed the man's address. I took a cab over there and the same lady greeted me at the door. I bullshitted my way in by saying I was with the "Traffic

Fatality Division." We talked for a while and she really opened up. I took her out to dinner and we ended up by sleeping together early in the morning.

DALLAS, TX—I was doing my laundry when this tall cowboy in very tight clothes (his wash-day spares) started banging on a washing machine that had eaten his quarters. The other patrons looked very concerned, almost terrified. I pointed out to the cowboy an "out of order" sign on the machine he was attempting to use and I guided him to one that worked. He tipped his hat to me.

PHOENIX, AZ—Patrick had lived out here in the early nineteen-seventies and he still labors under the delusion that it remains some sort of frontier settlement. He had voted "no" on the proposed Martin Luther King holiday. "We didn't need another day off and we didn't want to import your problems from back east," he explained.

SAN DIEGO, CA—Ocean Beach stinks. Speed freaks settle down here like silt; skewered fish dragged behind golf carts. Patrick has just entered puberty, at the astonishing age of thirty-three. He fell in with a gang of dandies who roam the beaches here. They smoke glue mixed with crushed caffeine pills. They terrorize sunbathers by pulling their hair and running away. They crowd the karaoke bars and enter singing contests to earn money. Patrick finally met a good woman. He retreated with her into the mysteries of Kaballah. He couldn't decide if he wanted to be a theosophical fascist or a Jew but faith won out. In order to perfect himself for his beloved he underwent a procedure to re-attach his foreskin so it could be removed again at the *brit milah.* This added about two flapping inches to his penis size but did not impress the Rabbi who beseeched Patrick to study and prepare to face the *Bet Din* or else produce some apodictic genealogy.

SEATTLE, WA—There were a lot of homeless people here. Jill had been taking valium all day. She drove away from the curb while Patrick was still getting into the backseat. The door shut by itself a block down the street as we drove on. Patrick took a cab back to the hotel.

SAN FRANCISCO, CA—I met up with my pal Reggie. About a year ago he did a "green card" marriage with some chick here. He is from Indonesia, originally. She started spreading it around that Reggie had left her after a couple weeks and was living with some other girl. None of her friends knew that the whole thing was an immigration scam. They couldn't discover the truth; Reggie doesn't hang out, he has to work all the time. The chick started throwing benefit parties for herself to raise money for what she termed her "legal defense fund". Everyone believed Reggie to be a real third-world bastard who had abandoned his wife yet refused to dissolve the marriage because of his religious zealotry. He isn't like that at all. He works hard, reads the newspaper, does photography as a hobby. Yesterday, he took the streetcar downtown to see about a better job at another restaurant. Written on the chalkboard outside he saw: "Lupita Divorce Fund Benefit Tonight". He spoke to a woman there and got the story but she didn't know he was the husband.

DENVER, CO—There was a lot of rain here. An extremely skilled maintenance man fixed the heater in my hotel room. I admire people who enjoy their work and the pride of doing something well. The hotel management staff, by way of contrast, are restless and reluctant. Denver seems to have been settled by people who trekked out here, saw the Rocky Mountains looming before them and said: "Fuck it, this is far enough." With the heater going full blast I took a nap and woke up sweating from a dream where crowds shrieked down the street in panic. I turned on the television and every channel was showing some bombed out federal building in Oklahoma City. Early reports blamed Islamic enemies but Jill and I surmised it was the work of domestic terrorists; it's the anniversary of the Waco thing.

DETROIT, MI—They need to get gambling legalized here. Maybe to satisfy the need for modesty they could have casino dirigibles circling the sky above the city.

TORONTO, ONT—A kid behind me at the Blue Jays' baseball game was hit with a foul ball. He had a seizure. They should have shown it on the jumbo-tron, it was very exciting. Astroturf, which I had never seen before, is basically just green carpeting. It reminded me of when my brother and I would play baseball in the house.

CHICAGO, IL—I threw the lid of a takeout cup of cappuccino off the hotel balcony. It landed on a woman's head and stuck to her hair. I called out to her but she didn't respond.

EL PASO, TX—We flew down to the border. I was exhausted when I got to the hotel. I watched television in a half-slumber. When the Juarez, Mexico station signed off a jarring brass refrain woke me and I saw a hawk and a golden sphere. I thought, "No more leave to be American." I kept the test pattern on and called Patrick to come over to my room. Evaluating subtle changes in repetition can be made stronger by sharing. Sharing enriches the ineffable, frustrating control of the infinitely predictable. If things keep going on this way I will eventually escape into silence and isolation. Being very strong and determined I would find that certain kind of religion which offers salvation from mistakes without having to admit mistakes. Confession can be embarrassing. I prefer the transitional state where cause and effect become mutually blunted and give rise to an orderly kind of peace to which no debts are owed.

TULSA, OK—The toilet backed up in Jimmy's hotel room so he burned incense to cover the smell. He wouldn't come downstairs and drink with us at the bar because he had seen a kid down in the lobby earlier carrying a gun. The lobby smelled like oil.

NEW ORLEANS, LA—The heat was so deep here, the humidity transported me to a stellar plane; it was spiritual elixir. I was about to give some money to a bum on the street. He was in a wheelchair. A cop pulled up and said, "Don't feed the animals. He got that way jumping out of a window during a drug bust."

PITTSBURGH, PA—During the long drive here we stopped at a place where they were still flying the confederate stars and bars. The waitress could tell we were Yankees so she purposely fucked up our order; she served Jimmy a beer mixed with lemonade when he had asked for a bourbon. The plates of food were rotten and I figured out pretty quickly what was going on. For some reason Patrick was oblivious and he ate his hotdogs in spite of our warnings. I left a tip of 13 pennies, one for every state in the original CSA (counting the governments-in-exile of Missouri and Kentucky). An hour later, we were stuck on a bridge in a traffic jam behind a wrecked trailer and Patrick got hit with food poisoning. There was nowhere to go so he had to shit in a cardboard box in the back seat. In Pittsburgh, I left my watch in the hotel room but the maid scrupulously recovered it and the manager agreed to send it ahead to Philadelphia.

WHEELING, WV—As we were walking into a bar Jimmy informed me that a man had been shot there the night before. On the way back to the hotel a white car was following us. I stopped by the river to piss and the white car roared past us. The occupants: three teenage girls.

PROVIDENCE, RI—I have reached the point where I can't sleep unless I tip over the tables in the hotel room and use them to block the windows and doors.

BALTIMORE, MD—My driver needed to stop off and buy himself a new watch. His old watch was stuck on military time and the alarm would go off randomly.

WASHINGTON, DC—Jill told me a terrible story about her cousin, Mike. The kid was a professional singer. He did weddings, reunions, nightclubs; there was good money in it. Mike joined a group called "The Flashpoint" who played fifties and sixties hits for the old people. Over the summer the guy whom Mike had replaced as singer killed his girlfriend and himself in an ether and cocaine delirium. He had murdered her with a dull kitchen knife but used a gun on himself. The scene was horrendous and so it got a lot of attention in the local news. One paper called up the manager of "The Flashpoint" and requested a publicity photo which was duly sent along. The newspaper ran Mike's picture, complete with ruffled velvet tux and theatrical grin, alongside the story of the murder. The headline: "Singer for Local Musical Group in Drug-Fuelled Murder/Suicide."

PHILADELPHIA, PA—My watch was returned to me but I found out that my sick cat at home died last night.

6

MY TV DON'T WORK NO MORE

It's been a rough year for me, I don't mind telling you. I wish I had eye-glasses an inch thick but they don't make them anymore. Everything tends to the streamlined now. Even the most lascivious or obese fellow might appear stylish and in the game. All year, all these women have been trying to skin me, so I had to take a few months of respite on the couch. And when I'm on the couch, I watch TV.

Most television these days is made for the all-important busy and productive viewer. Niche tastes have proliferated to such an extent that channel surfing has become a laborious task that requires attentive research. Viewing choices have narrowed from a plural vision of the entirety into a fragmented Babel of direct marketing. Every choice is focused in a sliver-slim two-way peephole baring but a single element of the whole. In the past, the formally limited three network valve filtered all efforts directed into the clutch of televised media and revealed so much more detail in a simplistic and highly refined monument of explicative images. A vast resource of useful information was hidden within the multi-colored video bands, revealed in abstract and cold solidity each night after Carson and the National Anthem closed out the programming day. A sustained wail blared infernally along with the test pattern of rectangular stripes and ushered in the timeless period of meditation when the all-seeing eye rolled back into its head to re-energize by scanning the dreams of America. A sense of wide-spread reality could be divined from within this grotesque public sorcery. The Titans have since discovered that we are more than willing to design smaller aisles of content for them. They need only to control one of the tributaries of the big river. You call it choice; I call it "a cop on every corner."

It was hard to fall into a groove, there on the couch. I had to keep

checking the schedule and flipping around to piece together a sem-
blance of the programming day. It was late at night when I started to
watch re-runs of *Wings*, the sitcom that aired from 1990 to 1997. I have
now watched the entire run, and I believe that *Wings* represents a critical bridge from the past television paradigm. *Wings* addresses much of
the confusion and sickening vulnerability that ushered in the abuses of
our current "on-demand" system. It also demonstrates a crucial lesson
about struggling to make clear choices in a world where selfish and
sensation-absorbed insularity is encouraged.

The series begins with a premise: Two brothers are reunited after
their father's death because his will forces them to do so. Joe (played
by Tim Daly) is an orderly hometown boy running a small commuter
airline in Nantucket. His younger brother Brian (Steven Weber) is a
feckless and irresponsible layabout who ran off with Joe's wife years
before and has been drifting around the Bahamas. They are both
pilots. It comes about that Brian has been dumped by Joe's ex-wife and,
upon returning home, is invited to stay and fly planes for Joe's airline,
Sandpiper Air. Initially, the two brothers compete for the affections
of Helen Chappell (Crystal Bernard), a formerly obese childhood
friend who is now beautiful. She runs the lunch counter in the small
Tom Nevers airfield, where most of the action of *Wings* takes place.
Helen speaks in a thick Southern accent, which is explained away in
passing—something to do with moving back to Texas for a time. She
plays the cello and dreams, off and on, of leaving for greater career
opportunities.

Eventually, Joe and Helen begin a relationship that breaks apart
and resolves over the course of the series. This leads to the introduc-
tion of two female characters as foils to Brian. Alex (Farrah Forke)
is a strong-willed and glamorous helicopter pilot. She departs and is
replaced by Helen's prissy and demanding sister Casey (the brilliant
Amy Yasbeck), who returns to the island after being dumped by her
husband. There is a stable ensemble of town denizens, including the
grotesque Roy Bigguns, a dumb mechanic, an old woman and an
Italian cabdriver.

The premise was diminished soon into the series' run. Theatrical
convention such as dramatic polysemy, bathos and farce was the true

foundation of *Wings*. By building the show on this tradition, *Wings* never put its faith or hope for survival in the potential of its characters or premise. Rather, *Wings* changed dynamics and destroyed its own credibility with each passing episode. It responded to trends and styles. Since it was built on the classical fundamentals of comedy merely adorned by the conventions of the sitcom, the wavering attractiveness of the lead characters and the disposability of their goals never hurt the potential for comedy to damage their lives without remission. *Wings* accumulated comic situations but not the restraints imposed by the management of a consistent tone. For example, *Seinfeld* had always to maintain a certain formulaic distance from the conventions of a premise-based show such as *I Dream of Jeannie* and could never resort to dramatic character interaction.

Wings, however, could flirt with whatever tone would lend itself to satisfying humor, whether it meant posing dramatic choices that grew out of character development or rationing out jokes to the characters as types within the predictable limitations of a weekly sitcom. Unlike realistic sitcoms such as *Roseanne* or *The Cosby Show*, it was possible for *Wings* to explode the boundaries of premise temporarily without having to rationally explain the alteration. The characters on *Wings* often mention past events, but no matter how severe the comedic damage might be, it is absorbed back into the characters as they fight always to return to the banality they claim to despise.

When *Roseanne* won the lottery, this exploding of the entire framework of her show diminished its strength by removing the limitations of the characters, who were merely revealed to be the same people-only with money. I enjoyed the brave self-destruction of this show, but the implosion was never complete. And it paled in comparison to the writing and ensemble acting of the early seasons that depicted such minute struggles and terrors as "Dan and Roseanne can't find time to have sex" or "Jackie slept with Arnie." The early character-driven comedy could even allow for dramatic episodes, like one in which Dan beats up Jackie's abusive boyfriend. The events always resolved back into the characters, but had to be carried forward as they grew because they were "real." When the family won the lottery, the characters grew at a realistic rate and the genius of the show resisted the absurdity imposed

upon it. Because *Wings* consistently undermined and even attempted
to destroy its characters, such sad events as infidelity, house fires, mental illness, death and plane crashes were handled on both a realistic
level (within the limited selfish natures of the characters) and on an
absurd level (by exploiting any possibility for a cheap joke).

The popular reality and acceptance of the lead characters derived
from the theatrical technique of the actors. Because the characters
were types alternately struggling against and embracing their mun-
danity, *Wings* used broad theatricality to communicate the characters'
inner lives. Expansive and optimistic behavior was consistently met
with crushing defeat. Watching the characters struggle under the
oppression of this justice makes their fates both sympathetic and satisfying. The characters are always actors and never hope to simulate a
family of ciphers that we must take into our hearts. *Wings* never valued
its characters over a joke. This can be a killing flaw in most sitcoms, as
the characters must possess some sort of iconic power to keep the show
alive long after the formula becomes tired. *Wings*, however, started out
tired, stayed tired and prospered.

The consummate theatrical skill of the supporting actors was critical to the show's success. Thomas Haden Church played Lowell, the
mechanic. In his exaggerated garb of jumpsuit, tool belt and cap he
was the Schneider, or Rerun, of *Wings*. Lowell provided non sequitur
responses, slapstick physical japes and "stupid" misreadings of reality.
Rebecca Schull played Fay, the aged attendant at the Sandpiper Air
counter, an ex-stewardess from the golden days of aviation and the
widow to three husbands named George. With her pleasing matronly
ways, she provided opportunity for situations based on age stereotypes
and jokes in the form of inappropriately devilish comments which con-
tradicted her appearance. Tony Shalhoub, an American of Lebanese
descent, played the doomed Italian cabdriver Antonio in the broadest
possible accent. Shalhoub has not been typecast or trapped forever in
this role (unlike Costanza or Cliff the Postman) both because of this
simple distancing device and the cumulative effect of the repellent
aspects of the show as a whole. Whereas "Costanza" is a tour-de-force
performance that created an inescapably iconic identity for the actor
Jason Alexander, "Antonio" is a tour-de-force of acting that distanced

Tony Shalhoub from the character by distancing the character from the audience.

Television is a wasteland of unintended consequences and love flows to the most unlikely flaws within the attractive whole, creating in memory a monument devoid of details. If a show becomes popular to the point of defining its viewers' identities, all action within the structure is unfailing until it loses its audience. *Wings* avoided this burden throughout its run. Although nothing makes sense like success, it remains to be judged if such unflagging identification has egregious effects. Allegorically, the process seems destructive and Tony Shalhoub's characterization (and *Wings* as a whole) suggests a method of challenging predetermination, fate and oblivion.

Wings is a compendium of such circular allegory, a closed network that contains and accidentally reveals stunning details through its efforts to retain a successful structure. It reduces the old form of television as an entity into one show. Sadly, it is an Ouija board that speaks only of the past but when I had completed the course of the show I was still able to lift myself off the couch and overcome the deliberation that had been afflicting me. The debilitation I had imagined was replaced by a method of perception both artificial yet efficacious; a simulacra that imitated the process that *Wings* applied to the inherent reflexivity of television. When a show (or an entire network) focuses narrowly on a single subject such as the houses of celebrities or the remodeling of an old motorcycle, this negating stricture precludes any helpful revelations which can only come when a presiding body attempts to read the common mind. The narrow focus shields a controlling entity from revealing more than desired. There can never be a *Wings* network, but if competition in the cable and broadcast industry is ever wisely reformed, the utilitarian potential of television could be restored. Our current plight might be viewed as only a transitional phase—a phase that *Wings* both predicted and reflected but never presumed to resolve.

7

DRUGS

Rick and Buzzard sat in a restaurant booth on a Tuesday. Lunch had been ordered and Rick started in on an Arab kid sitting at the counter.

"Look at that idiot. He's sitting pretty close," Rick said.

"He looks wasted; mechanical retribution by chemicals. Just stick it in and who knows where you're going. Sex is weak by comparison, painful, controllable. Drugs give more than organization or reward; some people find wonder in them. They make a mystery out of it. They won't wait around for someone to show them something. They just put themselves under and go; they test it out, " Buzzard said.

"I'm off that wheel. Spare me the details of the world at large today. The Arabs are punks and Israelis are nobly deluded. We'd be in there in a flash if we could drill for oil under the temple mount. The whole thing ruins so many good magazines I have to read comic books at the dentist now. The extrusion of religion back into politics was too well-managed. Meanwhile, there's pleasure beating through the world under everything—throb, throb, throb; we do what we like to do. Why do anything else?"

"The ancient saints, the amazing ones like Saint Jude, that's far away from us; what's amazing to me is that glass crater from the atom bomb. The saints can't give to me anymore. There are some people lucky enough to live in a world of miracles."

The loud Tejano music distracted Buzzard and he stopped. He turned to the miniature jukebox in the booth and flipped through it to find the song that was playing.

"Here it is," Buzzard continued. "That singer Selena had the misfortune of being a saint somewhere out there in the unmade population. She worked in the lives of peasants; out at the rodeo."

"She had a fat ass," Rick said.

"We don't know that, you're thinking of the actress that played her in the movie."

"She had one, too."

"You know, the other day my kid got sick at school and I skipped an important meeting to pick him up. That's the sort of thing that a man does now," Buzzard said.

"That and masturbate," Rick added.

"It's all about the family."

"I am talking to Saint Kleen."

"He was a holy man."

"I haven't had sex in three weeks so that should count for something," Rick said. He slid a dollar into the jukebox, flipped a few racks and found his number. A Spanish tenor voice drifted from the speakers. Rick sang along in English, "A sad story of one . . . who will do again the things . . . so many times done . . . when it fails again . . . I take no blame . . . if it wasn't for them . . . something, something. Sentimental torture, people love that."

"Know your enemy," Buzzard said.

"There is no greater concern," Rick agreed.

"What about the fragile mountains? The spirits of the land? The dying seas?"

"I don't feature a change of priority. There's no reason to change when we hold all the cards. And we will still strike first."

"They have no chance?" Buzzard asked.

"No." Rick sliced his forefinger across his neck. The waitress brought the trays. Rick ate slowly. Buzzard watched and coughed once while balling up a napkin.

"My story takes place in a log home. Let's say in Oregon," Buzzard began.

"All right, Oregon it is."

"The father enters. He's cut down the very last tree in the forest and now he can move to the city and drink whiskey. His son, Steve, walks in dressed up as his son Paul.

Steve says, 'Now that the forest is clear I can sleep without worrying about wolves.'

The father says, 'We all win.'

Steve asks, 'What do I win?'

The father answers him, 'You won't have to worry about wolves anymore.'

The second son, Paul, comes in dressed as a wolf. He says, 'I'm not a real wolf. I'm better than a real wolf. I don't have an odor. I don't need to reproduce.'

The third son, Jack, flies into the room carried aloft by a flock of birds.

The father says, 'Those must be all the birds from the forest. They have nowhere to roost now that the trees are gone. I need my gun.' The father waves his gun around. He stirs up all the birds and they fly around the room in a panic.

The mother comes in. She says, 'Put that gun away!'

The father says, 'I need it. Look at these birds!'

The birds are attacking, thrashing the wood and windows.

The fake wolf says, 'Don't fire that gun in here!'

The father fires the gun inside the small cabin, trying to kill the birds."

"That's the story," Rick said. He pushed his plate away and looked over his shoulder at the counter. He pretended to wave for the waitress and eyed the Arab kid at the same time. The kid didn't seem to be watching them.

Buzzard counted on his fingers for a moment. "That leaves five people dead, in total."

"Dressed up in fancy costumes, dressed like a wolf, dead birds everywhere; not that he was able to shoot them all."

"It doesn't look good if that's all there is to find; no note, no survivor to tell the story, no explanation and a lot to explain," Buzzard concluded.

"Like the Chicago baby that died one night in 1957. The mother was poor and young, she sticks him in a shoebox under the floor," Rick pointed his fork downwards.

"Forty years later they find the box, the past speaks grimly again as always."

"The way things will happen when we are among them, there will always be a reasonable explanation and motivation," Rick said.

"Is he looking over here?" Buzzard pointed towards the Arab kid.

"No."

"Keep talking and watch him." Buzzard was irritated.

"If something happens now that we didn't predict, it must have emerged from the past, from across that dark line." Rick tried to distract him.

"People love that shit," Buzzard said.

When Rick and Buzzard left the restaurant the Arab kid, Bedu, followed them for a couple blocks and watched them go up Secor Avenue. He turned back towards Gordon's Gym. Bedu had seen them before, watching Leroy Dugan work out a few weeks ago. From the look of them and the way they talked he figured they worked for Interest Outreach. Bedu had wanted to get a telephone job there but they hated everybody except blacks and whites; just the so-called old neighborhood people could work there. It was a good job, he'd heard, just reading off of a sheet, no selling. Doesn't matter, he thought, the gym was much better for him and he had a lot of friends there.

If they were interested in the Dugan fight that meant they would bet money on it. No matter what politics they took, whomever they served, if there was a promising local fighter coming up they would want to become involved. Pretty soon, if the fighter was good, he'd be out of here and on to bigger things. For now, the kid was local, the money was manageable, the possibilities untouched. There was great power in seeing it from the beginning.

If they were interested in Dugan then Gordon would want to know and he'd thank Bedu for looking out. Around the crew at the gym, Bedu felt safe. Past the doors, through the cold weight room all lost their arrogance when faced with such human beauty. Bedu himself did not fight but he was a man near the men in the ring. He took orders from the trainers and did not question them. Before he started coming here there used to seem only brutality from which he hid or brutality that protected him. He had learned that the fight was more complex than he had understood. Two strong forces at war were attracted to each other like lovers.

He once watched a fly dart around two sparring boxers. The gym had a lot of cracked screens and in the summertime Bedu was assigned to spray for bugs and hang up strips. He developed an eye for fast moving insects. The fly gracefully traced through the movements of the fighters' arms and bodies. It dodged every swing and step while seeking to rest on one man's slick forearm. The boxers were generating currents of air. The fly would be pulled in but ride out on a wave and return from above. The fly was never killed. When one boxer went down hard the fly landed on his shoulder for a few minutes and then flew off to a window.

While those two men were teaching each other about fighting Bedu was watching the way they admired each other and did not swing wildly to exterminate everything near them. Power showed generosity by its self-absorption. Away from the ring, Bedu still respected the cruder view he had been taught to live for so long. He had seen too many good dog fights. That was still the rule, sometimes things had to get vicious, the weak were discarded as a charm to keep wholesale death at bay. He would need to learn carefully or he would still be prey, killed because he was still essentially weak. A few minutes after the sparing session had ended, Bedu hunted down the fly and smacked it with a newspaper.

With his lunchtime work completed, Rick arrived back at the shop. The Interest Outreach office was empty but for the floor manager. Rick handed in his receipts.

"Cunningham wants to see you, so stick around," the floor manager said.

"Is that who I think it is in that frame?" Rick asked.

"That man is Franklin Roosevelt."

"Is that a joke? 'At exactly nine this morning, by the fire, you fear not the fear, of a brand new deal.' "

"It's not a joke and that's not pulling him down good."

"He abandoned the Jews," Rick reminded him.

"It's easy to look back and say that kind of thing. If you don't want a human in charge you can worship Ronald Reagan. He was perfect."

"Roosevelt couldn't walk. They'd prop him up so he didn't look weak."

"They were working with a real man. I can't say he won the war but I learned from my grandfather the kind of bond he had with the people."

"It was your grandfather who taught you about Roosevelt?" Rick asked.

"He brought history into my life. I wanted to learn more about it. I couldn't understand, at first, but I kept looking."

"There had to be something to it," Rick said.

"That's right. If it meant that much to him, there had to be something to it," the floor manager explained.

Cunningham, the boss, played with his watch. A watch, foremost for him, had to be submersible. It had to have a lot of features. At times like this, Rick focused on one telling word or motion. He could not be distracted by any movement or energy directed to him.

"You saw Buzzard?" Cunningham asked.

"I did. I taped the whole conversation."

"He talk a lot?"

"He's high strung. I think we can work with him."

"We need someone like Buzzard on staff."

"He's high strung," Rick said.

"Did you see Leroy Dugan?"

"A fighter wouldn't be eating lunch there."

"He's quick, that Dugan." The boss punched the air.

"Sure, he's quick. He's still small."

"He's beautiful, don't worry about that. These little watch buttons are driving me crazy, to use the stopwatch I have to push a bunch of them just right. I can't use this thing when I'm driving."

"How about getting a Cartier?" Rick suggested.

"Why don't I just hang a sign around my neck that says, 'peanut-sized balls'?" The boss stopped jabbing his watch. He stood up and walked closer to Rick. "This assignment is a big break for us. I don't want you sending things uptown to Pitt without going through me."

"They hired all of us."

"It looks better. It makes us seem more professional for everything to come through me."

"I understand, as long as you're giving us an even split."

"The pay stays the same." The boss let his watch hand drop to his side but did not look away from Rick's face. "We should look at Gordon's Gym. Gordo's a stand-up guy but the place is just lousy with Arabs. Pitt feels that if we dig around about their visas we'll come up with something."

"I know Dugan's trainer. There's an Alcoholics Anonymous meeting he goes to at the church. I can work on him."

"If we can get this done for Pitt I think we can get a much bigger grant next year." The boss started examining his watch again.

"It's an important job," Rick said. "People won't like the idea of a bunch of Muslims working in a big gym down here without visas."

"You got it. You're doing great. This is going to make us legitimate where it counts."

"We're a good team." Rick wanted to keep the conversation going.

"Do your part and we'll all win," Cunningham added.

Rick observed the polite routines as he left the office but he knew it was a bad deal. When telling lies the boss stopped playing with his watch. It had always been that way and the prospect of a new dose of clean money could not conceal it.

"You're Arab, so you're Muslim?" Caldera asked.

"I'm not anything. I was raised Christian." Bedu was cleaning out the lockers.

Caldera was the trainer who took on all the boys who showed promise. It was a bitter prospect since the good fighters would leave him if they ever got the chance to move up. If they were good, the fighters would be swept into the realm of bigger agents, dismiss Caldera and leave this crumbling gym. To Caldera, such consistently poor treatment was the final, damning piece of evidence that proved he was a failure in the science of boxing.

Leroy Dugan was with him now and the Dugan project gave Caldera every right to stride around the gym proudly. He could put on the same beaten pants and shoes every day, take lunch with the neighborhood businessmen, discuss training with the Chinese across town. Caldera had every right to these luxuries as long as he worked in Dugan's corner, shouting unintelligible commands and rocking against the corner pole with a simulated intensity inspired by his frequent migraine headaches. There were also the weekly Alcoholics Anonymous meetings at the big church in the center of the gym's district. The meetings were not attended anonymously, Caldera made his membership plain to everyone he could. It was like being in the chamber of commerce.

After shooting out the transom windows in the locker room five years ago he had forced one of his pugilists down to the tiles, with an empty and warm pistol as persuasive aid. Caldera had grabbed a weight bar off the rack and beaten the young man. This young man was about to leave the gym and enter the employ of a big promoter. The assault had been thorough and the placement of the blows exacting. The young man was rendered stupid and could not remember who had attacked him. Today, the kid fetched things for local fight fans around town who cursed this accidental theft of promise and mournfully extended charity to him. This respite from a worse fate had been brought about only through Caldera's intervention. Had it not come, the kid would have been hurt badly by much better athletes and would have ended his days in a penitentiary. After this episode, Caldera publicly declaimed his problems with drink and added Alcoholics Anonymous to his weekly schedule of appearances. The meetings helped him to control his indulgence. Caldera abstemiously observed a medicinal regimen of gin to keep his blood sugar in balance and his mind well-equipped.

The incident had forced Caldera to reconsider some elements of his training method and when Dugan came to him Caldera was careful. Beyond training the young horse in the rudiments, he also formulated a plan that would keep himself indispensable to Dugan's future. There was no doubt that the boxer's physical ability would bring reward. Before that starlight was unleashed, Caldera sought to penetrate the needs of the young man. Dugan might move away from the gym and into the world of success but Caldera would be going with him.

Rick marveled that he had been able to hold himself in front of his boss. With every glance at that moron's watch, Rick had increased the total amount of funding he planned to divert into his own pocket. Long years of patience would guide Rick's actions.

He remembered exactly the moment when he had discovered this skill of immunity: riding in a black car, heading into town, ten years past. His girlfriend wore a black leather dress. His disinterest had been mounting for weeks as her commercial interest in sexuality emerged, in its most uncannily standard form. In the car Rick mentioned he had spoken to a friend of his who had the annoying habit of describing in detail the symptoms and repercussions of chronic and severe hemorrhoids.

His girlfriend launched into her act. She let her thighs gnaw against the car seat as she drawled out the fantasy, "He calls you all the time. I know he's gay. He wants you to go down on him. He wants you to go down on his hemorrhoids." She flexed her shoulders causing her earrings to slap her neck. "I'd go down on him. I'd bet you'd like to watch."

Rick leaned away from her. Pretending to be embarrassed, he said flatly, "That's terrible. Stop it." He never rode in a car with her again and soon shook her loose.

That skill of response had served him since. It was smart not to point out vulnerability when people presented such thin fronts. Working for Cunningham had been easy, until today. By the disgust it had inspired, today's speech had started the clock; Rick was no longer immune.

Caldera was alone outside the church when Rick arrived.

"Rick, you're one of us?" Caldera shouted.

"One of what?" Rick asked.

"Fuck it." Caldera looked up and down the street. "I'm waiting for this guy. He owns three shoe stores in town and he loves Dugan. I was hoping to hit him up for a nice pair, something leather."

"Are you getting sponsorships for your fighters?"

"For me! Dugan gets nothing. That boy is going to stay starving. He will smile for a spoonful of salt. This is the way it can work. If a neighborhood kid has promise he gets out of here, that isn't right."

"My boss likes Dugan, too."

"I'm sure he's looking forward to the fight. Maybe some of these fat guys will figure out that we should put Dugan under contract before someone else grabs him. They all seem to have plenty of cash to play with; they should put some of it to something serious."

"They don't care. They like the association, the excitement but they lack patience. They wouldn't trust you with the money," Rick explained.

"They don't know anything. I'm not worried, I've gotten wise. Leroy Dugan will be taking me with him."

"Don't set yourself up. You're too old for that bullshit."

Caldera was enraged, "I take this seriously and I'm the only one. I have control of this kid. I'm not going to leave this up to money or chance."

"Relax, I'm not saying you can't do it."

"I'm saying I have done it. I'm closer to that kid than his own skin." Caldera laughed bitterly. "I'm under his skin. By the time he decides he wants me out, it'll be too late. I'm certain he'll try and dump me eventually but not before I get my piece. I am owed for a lot of kids and Leroy Dugan is going to pay. He won't be able to fight without me. I can tell you this much, I am indispensable to him."

"So, what should I tell my boss about the fight?" Rick asked.

"Tell him Dugan is a lock. And remind your boss, after the fight, which trainer it was who put all the money back into his pocket."

"Sounds good," Rick said.

Bedu wiped the back of Leroy Dugan's neck. The fighter spit on the floor. Dugan had looked good in today's workout but now Bedu noticed he seemed restless. "Are you thinking about the fight?" Bedu asked.

"I don't think of it," Dugan said.

If Bedu could know what the fighter thought it would help his own education. He hadn't yet learned one thing this way from any fighter. Everyone else could talk about it but that was useless to Bedu. He watched the fights in silence and they stayed that way in memory. The trainer told the boxer what to do, the boxer agreed. The boxers liked to talk about other things.

"How long before the fight do they give drug tests?" Dugan asked. "I heard they take blood and test it. When do they do that?"

"The bout is sanctioned. They examined you and you made your weight."

"Sure, sure."

"In this state they don't test for drugs. Maybe if they were suspicious they might test after the fight. Did Caldera show you the entry form? It says that testing *may* be used. Our gym has a good reputation, Gordon is strict about things."

"How much am I getting paid, if I win?" Dugan asked.

"You can't get paid. You would lose your amateur status. You couldn't fight in the Olympics," Bedu said, teasing him.

"Do they still fight naked at the Olympics?" Dugan asked.

"No," Bedu said.

"I feel a little run down. I should go talk to Caldera." Dugan grabbed his robe and left the locker room.

Buzzard noticed the Arab kid sitting at the counter as he and Rick ate at a booth in the restaurant. "That kid is crawling up my 'blank'."

"I'll take Brett Somers," Rick said.

"She was my favorite *Match Game* panelist," Buzzard said.

"That show ran on booze. It had to, they taped seven of them every day."

"It was all improvised, they wouldn't redo anything," Buzzard elaborated.

"People don't conflict that way in public anymore."

"Where can people gather now to touch a part of themselves and conflict with others to include self-interest into the commonplace?" Buzzard asked.

"At the movies, at the strip joint," Rick suggested.

"But they're like graveyards; side by side and solitary."

"While silence spreads to incorporate by the common goal of binding. A detached element merely coexists in an unresolved state," Rick said.

"We need to resolve that," Buzzard said.

"The disparate elements can't be in conjunction?"

"Unless they are collected into the whole they are out of tune."

"A social metaphor?"

"We need to reduce things to general heads," Buzzard pronounced.

"I saw a woman with fine-rimmed sunglasses, a lightly weathered face; she was explaining the quality and variety of olive oil. She had contempt for those who would consume bad oil."

"My mother had a cap of wiry hair, a pink sweat suit. She could explain the poses, the colors and craft in any cement garden ornament. She had contempt for the wrong ornament in the wrong place," Buzzard countered.

"Everyone has their boundary."

"It's what distinguishes them from the disparate. The search for purity relieves the common feelings of base need."

"It's inescapable, no matter to what rhythm one adheres. There's an invariably strict relationship to an irreducible center."

"That kid is watching us again," Buzzard said.

"He's no trouble."

"I'm a sociopath but you are an acute sociopath. I feel like I'm always going to be on the losing end with you."

"Your losing streak is over. Cunningham wants you to join Interest Outreach. In fact, you'll be taking over my position."

"Are you getting kicked upstairs?" Buzzard asked.

"Something like that," Rick said.

Again, Bedu followed the two men as they left the restaurant. When Rick walked alone he turned and watched the kid. Bedu did not hesitate. He caught up with Rick and greeted him.

"You were making my friend nervous in there," Rick said. "I could tell you wanted something this time."

"My name is Bedu. I work at Gordon's Gym. I wanted to talk to you about the fight this weekend."

"Did Caldera send you?" Rick asked.

"I'm working for myself," Bedu said.

"Why would you think I care about that fight?"

"You work at Interest Outreach, you have to care. I know something and I'm going to tell you. I heard you speaking to that guy. I think you deserve to hear what I have to say. I can't claim I understood all of your conversation but enough of it seemed to be transplanted from a place where I would like to be; there is an explanation for what will come to pass and I feel like you were asking me to divulge, you were warning me that possessing this information, solitary, would be too much for my station. First, can you explain what it was that you and that man were talking about?"

"When a person hears words describing things which don't exist on the immediate horizon they might properly assume the speaker to be a fool. Why would you make the mistake of discounting your own eyes?"

"I see that you have money, you come and go as you please. I'm on a leash, the slightest tug I must obey. I don't have the correct words to escape it. I can't fight my way free; in my imagination, I put the world through its paces and imitate the gracefulness of the fights I have witnessed but I cannot turn these pictures into actions for myself. When I hear the conversations coming from your table in the restaurant, the words describe exactly the patterns I devise. You're not discussing boxing. I don't know what you are talking about and it would help me to learn. I will tell you what I know."

"I understand. You know you aren't the kind of person who would normally be given this education. You should have to live with those pictures in your head for the rest of your miserable life. You shouldn't be allowed to make the crucial links, or to use that algebra to commit mayhem. You were meant to die unfulfilled."

"Was it algebra that you were talking about? That comes from Arabs."

"In a way, I suppose it was; it is a code we speak. Maybe the words match the fights running through your head, maybe you cracked the code."

"I go everywhere in that gym, no one pays any attention to me. I watch everything closely."

"I'll make a deal with you. If you tell me what you know about the fight I will help you out. I'll get you into the ring. You have to recognize that it is all as real as a fist to the eye even when it feels like nothing. Maybe you're ready to be a fighter."

"I don't want charity," Bedu said. "You know that Caldera would kill Leroy Dugan before letting him go. That's why he has a plan working to keep the kid. The old man won't let it happen again; to be certain, he has been shooting Dugan up with cocaine for the past year.

Dugan is alone in the world and very stupid. He thinks he has been getting steroid shots. The cocaine keeps Dugan unraveled; he gets confused and agitated unpredictably. Then he goes to the old man for more shots. Caldera holds it back sometimes, rewards him, overdoses Dugan a little to make him sick. Dugan could have been a great fighter but he is used up. This weekend, Dugan will need so much cocaine in his system to get through the fight that he will not only lose but he'll probably be finished, his heart could explode in the third round."

"You can't intervene. I think you are smart enough to handle what is going to come your way; it was smart of you to tell me," Rick said.

"I hope that in return you'll give me what I need," Bedu said.

"We have a deal," Rick said.

Rick laid out a story for his boss, Cunningham, "Pitt is going to be pleased. The immigration beef is just the beginning. I got to someone on the inside, an Arab kid who cleans up around the gym. He was scared enough to talk. Right in our own neighborhood, a nest of towel heads are running drugs through Gordon's Gym. They get it from the Dominicans, sell it out of the gym, wash it up and give it over to Islamic charities. You know what that means."

"I'm shitting myself, Rick. This is the real dope, I'm overwhelmed," Cunningham said.

"Buzzard was instrumental in this. You were right about him."

"Pitt will be doing back flips over this motherfucker. I wouldn't doubt that we'll even get to take part in the investigation. We could be working with the District Attorney's office."

"I wouldn't deal you a weak hand," Rick said. He pulled out a portable recorder and set it down on the desk. "Listen to this."

The distorted sounds of a restaurant crowd played for a few seconds. Against a calmer background a voice spoke, it was Bedu talking on the street, "I work at Gordon's Gym. I know what money pass everywhere in that gym. The old man has been working with cocaine for the past year. In his system, the money goes to Arabs' charity. I watch everything closely."

Cunningham slapped the top of his desk. "Jesus, Ricky! All praise to fucking Allah. I'm taking that to Pitt on Monday."

"Bring me with you," Rick suggested.

"I explained about that. We need to present this in a simple way, one man; that would be me. I'll let him know you did the field work. He'll know how instrumental you are. We need to show a clear, professional face. That's my job, I handle public relations." The boss leaned down below the desk and emerged with two stacks of cash.

"I'll take my money now," Rick said.

"You got it. I'm sure you want to put something down on the fight for yourself. Let's also invest a little public funding into our boy, Dugan. I saw his workout yesterday. After you told me how Caldera is staking everything on him, I had to see it for myself. He was a tiger. Dugan is on his way up. It's too bad for Caldera, he'll get dumped. Gordon's Gym will be in the shit after we launch this investigation. We should try and enjoy this weekend." The boss handed five-thousand dollars to Rick.

Rick slipped the cash into his backpack.

"I don't care about losing that cash. We're buying community good-will. Dugan losing that way only makes it easier for us to bring the gym down. Where is Rick?" Cunningham pulled his feet off the desk and turned to watch Buzzard examining a row of plaques hanging on the wall.

"I don't know," Buzzard said. "He left me a message to come see you. God, that was a slaughter. I thought the kid was going to die."

"People love boxing around here but I can tell you that it is a bad business. The dog fights down on Bell Street are a better proposition. If a dog dies you just throw it in the river. The way that Dugan fell out, a fucking seizure seven minutes into a fight he should have ended in two minutes; there will be an investigation, they'll lose their license. Where the hell is Rick?"

"He called me from a mobile phone. Maybe he hit traffic." Buzzard tapped his finger on a framed snapshot of Cunningham with the mayor.

"Don't touch that, man. You look restless. You must want to get started. Go to the gym and grab the kid that Rick has under his fist. Do you know this kid?"

"I'd recognize the little prick."

"Check him out. I'm meeting with Pitt tonight. You couldn't have signed on at a better time, my man," the boss said.

"I appreciate the work. I don't know how you can stand being stuck in this office dealing with all those clowns, in the pictures here. It would drive me nuts," Buzzard said. He pulled his coat on and headed to the door.

"Everyone in their proper place. I'll wait around until Rick checks in; if you hear from him send him over. I think he took the fight to heart. I know he liked Dugan to go far, he was sentimental that way. Maybe he felt bad about the cash we lost. Tell him to forget it, there's a lot more coming once we get this thing set up. Tell him everything is peaceful and good."

"I will tell him." Buzzard departed, leaving the boss to wait unprofitably for Rick's return.

8

THE AMERICAN
ANTI-REVENANT LEAGUE

Not the strict definition of *revenant* (one who has returned in the form of a spirit or ghost); instead, specifically, a mortal, drained of their blood until dead, returning to assume the habitual practices of a vampire; someone living a lie until it becomes truth to them although it never becomes practically real.

A vampire knows to despise the revenant, one who joins the organization, cops the disguises, walks in the shadow of the damned, drinks blood from an obsidian goblet available for fifty dollars by mail order.

Indulgence and total suffusion can't bury or burn them, they are challenges to the revenant for desire is their perpetual mood. Revenants can only become reflections serially intersecting with the eventuality, the mystery; looking, searching, needing.

At a 1997 St. Louis Rams v. Washington Redskins NFL contest I counted five women with black eyes during one trip to the concession stand. The Redskins (the home team) were losing. One lone fan in a plastic yellow rain poncho, his face looking unformed from the brutal yet hard won sculptural redesign performed upon it during his own playing days, was attempting to rouse the crowd. He shouted: "the defense needs the crowd to be strong and loud." He waved his arms and exhorted us all to rise.

The revenant enjoys the taste of blood; to the vampire blood is a mere necessity. If humans believe they can influence the physical world through the psychic power of desire then, goddammit, they're mostly just going to get what they want.

LUCIFER: I like to get in there and I like to have them prove to themselves what they are capable of.

ME: The sincerity is certainly hilarious. Why are they obsessed with these cleansing transgressions? As they administer abuse are they not also absorbed and controlled by it? Why do they conspire with what overwhelms them? Why rape an old woman?

LUCIFER: They figure they win both ways, they transcend the common and they believe such acts impress me.

ME: Do they want to feel the way they imagine evil feels: powerful, focused, &c?

LUCIFER: Well, they feel they serve a higher power and it's one that answers their needs in a very direct fashion. I like to suggest more efficient methods for communicating their desires.

ME: They don't lack standards. These days, nominal psychic functions are pretty widely discussed; even accepted scientists look at the subject. If these were to become common human faculties would that worry you?

LUCIFER: That's not a problem for me, although that would mean entering an entirely different realm I'm sure the same desires would emerge relative to the transition. It's like, some would move up but also they'd be going to the back of a new line. My biggest gripe is with the flesh, anyway.

The problems arise in execution, crossing the chasm the revenant believes divides them from the perfection. Each step towards the image confounds and confuses the image; like a mirage, obviously.

The precise mind applied to musical organization, the sort of mind that finds fault with Louis Armstrong's music for its inherent contrapuntal mistakes, had one of its greatest full expressions with the mind of Marshall Applewhite, the leader of the Heaven's Gate UFO cult whose disciples killed themselves with poison applesauce in order to rendezvous with an invisible spaceship hiding in the tail of the Hale-Bopp comet. The steel-tense harmony of this former opera singer's system provides a simple lesson to us about the risks of paradigmatic transfer of symbolic logic systems to the social realm. This transfer is essential to the revenant. The world is filled with obstacles, questions and considerations; to get beyond them there must first be a metaphor.

"It's so simple, to go back is not the American Dream; it's not protection we need. The essence of it was space, yet the method was made flawed by space. The direction was outward from a light inside. Unfortunately, an image guided them; so fix that image and proceed with the method; don't forget to include something or someone in it. It must be wholly realized, think clearly about what is being created; don't just hammer something together which is merely acceptable and expedient. It was so simple."

AL JOLSON: That's pretty cute, kid, good work: "no easy answers"—that should be useful for knocking someone very stupid out of the box.

ME: If only Eddie Cantor had just once physically beat the shit out you . . . .

AL JOLSON: Pretty words and kisses on my rainbow-coalition-striped prostate. That little kike, Cantor, would sell his grand mammy's ass to a tubercular rag-picker for the chance to lick the juice off of my dick before the second matinee.

ME: That's right, you always had to ball a chorus girl or two before each of your shows; such energy!

AL JOLSON: That's goddam right, if I were working today I'd be a fucking universal titan. I'd be able to publicize the shit I did just to get off; the people would spontaneously reach into their vaults and shower me with diamonds to watch fifteen minutes of my life on television.

ME: You were Jewish; did you care about your religion?

AL JOLSON: Shut the hell up, you protestant pipsqueak. The way I figure it, if I were alive and working today I could instantly put five thousand little peasants like you out of business. I could cop your act in about two seconds, if I ever had the misfortune to witness it; then I'd probably fuck your mother and leave town.

ME: I liked that movie you did where you went to heaven in blackface and all the angels had blackface on and there was this little flying dog.

AL JOLSON: Why'd you have to bring that up? That was the lowest grossing picture of my career, almost killed me. Luckily, by then I was already a legend; there was nowhere to go after the moving pictures but to be paraded around like some hoary dignitary; more time for sex, so I couldn't complain.

ME: You would have to change your act to make it today.

AL JOLSON: No shit, again with the advice; naturally, you're missing the point: today it would be so much easier. With the energy I posses I would merely absorb a few base dreams and desires, pick off a few songs and be the first person to have sex in outer space on pay-per-view. The offstage stuff would galvanize my power base. When I think of all the time I wasted trying to hide all of that! I can dance and I'm white, keep it simple, give the people something they will take to heart. And once you have them don't take your eyes off them, keep that foot on their throat until they choke to death; nothing lasts forever.

ME: That seems sound.

AL JOLSON: I might also add "be yourself" but in your case, forget it.

It is exhausting trying to keep up with Jolson but he gives us the feeling that something big is coming around the corner—if we could just follow him until he leads us to where he's going. We could all be there, wiser, all together: ingenious Lucifer, the flying dog, Woody Hayes, the revered suicide, M. Blavatsky, and the revenant (miraculously mistaken for a vampire one night by a drunken Van Helsing, the revenant was given the honor of being beheaded and buried upside down, standing on the stump of his neck). We would be at the most glorious heights; for cannot the profundity of commitment be measured only in degrees of demonstration?

9

KARL MARX'S "18th BRUMAIRE"

In the annals of his many attempts at a new life this perhaps was one of the most ridiculous. He was stowed away in Iowa City in the poorly ventilated apartment of a young lady whom he had met at a local bar. He had since inched up with her to the point of planning to live with her here, in this town.

The season, a Midwestern summer, literally ascended from heavy weekend rains; what looked to be steam rose with the sun and surrounded the young woman's ill-prepared abode with a battery of thick reflected heat. After one attempt to walk outside at ten that morning he'd ruled the atmosphere unbearable and chose to sit down in the cool spot he had created by rolling away the rug in a windowless back room. He could touch the cold tiles and avoid the sunlight and humid clouds outside.

The woman had been gone for work since six. He had pretended to be asleep when she left and a phone message two hours later had informed him that she'd be working a double shift and would not return until eight o'clock that evening. He would be trapped inside all day without an air conditioner. The time had come to finally attack his copy of Karl Marx's *The 18th Brumaire of Louis Bonaparte* and read through it to set down some thoughts he'd been considering. He was better when he worked under pressure, physical pressure which exercised the imagination to calm the stress of the body. If thinking was not a struggle it seemed wasteful. As Marx said, "Men make their own history but not just as they please, they do it under circumstances directly encountered, given and transmitted from the past."

The hated weather and the crummy apartment provided the perfect opportunity to struggle against the tension of the last few weeks that had developed as he directed his thoughts towards a single goal, that being an alliance with a woman of some physical gifts, an honesty won by repeated exposure to the worst in life and a love of the pleasures of honest labor. In addition to whatever she might have decided to see in him he could offer to her an inability to exert any energy toward lying and the occasional check that would arrive for him at the post office box he had recently opened in town. Her apartment was not in town, he had no car and so he was trapped out in the woods where the weather seemed somehow more intense.

> "As unheroic as bourgeoisie society is it nevertheless took heroism, sacrifice, terror, civil war and battles to bring it into being." — *Karl Marx*

Some people are addicted to submerged conflict, they get lonely without it. He remembered the motto, "silence equals death." The marchers had used it to protest the presumed inaction of the government during the peak days of the AIDS epidemic. It resonated to many other kinds of paralysis. Even people with shattered nerves and the will to pacify enjoy feeling that conflict is impending or unavoidable; it's like the feeling of anticipation deep in the peace of the Grand Teton, the anticipation of the scream of a wild bird or the crash of a falling tree. It centers around the loneliness and the idea that loneliness or silence leads to death. The struggle to achieve a bourgeoisie dominated society must have been alluring because it first dictated conflict and chaos but the course of the disease led to full remission. Rather than struggling to consistently maintain the dormitive there would first be an inoculating struggle full of mayhem and noise which would later make victory feel like a bounty of peace where cowardice could flourish justifiably.

He had seen the "silence equals death" cipher a lot when he had lived in San Francisco. In a twisted sort of way it had been an exciting time back then. He'd had the lease on an apartment that cost about $650 a month and he had sublet half of it for $400 to a series of interesting but ephemeral types of the sort you would expect to encounter during the waning years of the Cold War.

There was one particular tenant, a man who had come up from San Diego in a black leather longcoat driving a revamped hearse. The tenant had brought his petite girlfriend, fussed over and cared for as though she were part of a doll collection, as well as a plan to head to the welfare office and apply for an ssi disability benefit on the basis of mental illness. Because San Francisco is both a city and a county it takes two shots of tax from everything and it was legend that if you could get on welfare you got paid double.

One afternoon, there had come a knock on the door. The cops and paramedics were responding to a planned overdose that the tenant had perpetrated. The tenant had related the details later while perched shirtless on a mattress, the stains from the charcoal he had been forced to swallow and spit up visible on his bare chest. Next day, the girlfriend had called the police to report a domestic assault. She had filled out a report which attributed the attack to her boyfriend's chronic depression. Such events would continue until the tenant figured a critical mass had been achieved and the time had come to submit to an evaluation.

During the final incident, he had been standing on the outside stairs while the tenant chased through the apartment like a lizard pursued by cops and paramedics. He had heard the tenant clamber up the fire escape and threaten to jump. The sound of bare skin dragging on gravel combined with the dull ring of cuffs and keys had flared briefly and then they had carried the tenant down the stairs past him.

As these events transpired, he had stood in the hall pretending to ring the bell of the stranger's apartment next door. All the while, he had mounted an impatient look on his face and checked his watch. The tenant had given him the thumbs up as the stretcher passed.

He never got his rent money that month. The tenant had come into his room and said: "I could have been approved but to get the check right away I have to go inside for thirty days because I may have overdone it a little. The person that gets the check for me has to be a relative but my girl and me aren't married. I filled out the forms incorrectly at the beginning, I should have requested another disability category. I changed my submission but it will take six weeks to process. In the meantime, she will apply; she has a cousin here that will act as her guardian for a cut. If you can give us some slack for a few weeks I'll give you three months rent all at once when we get the money." He had suggested to the tenant that something could be worked out.

He crept into the tenant's room later and grabbed the keys. While clutching a decorative samurai sword he had flipped on the lights and ordered them out. The tenant had made a move at him and he in turn had sliced at the loose part of the tenant's leather jacket. The sword pierced the material and lodged in the door frame. By brandishing the sword while kicking and cursing at them he had managed to move the two deadbeats down the hall and outside.

The next day, the tenant had come back with the cops, demanding the return of property. "You can't just keep their stuff, even if they're evicted and owe back rent. You have to go through the courts," the cop had said. He returned their few belongings including an inlayed wooden box which had held all the precious arrest reports and disability papers along with nine ceramic dolls, each with coloring, clothes and hair color to match the tenant's girlfriend.

However, Marx says, "Recollections of the past are drugs that can mask the reality of content." As human nature repeats predictably and simultaneously in a billion points on the globe every half-second (he imagined a time-lapse animation of a decaying dead rabbit with each spot of bacteria at work representing another opportunity for choice fulfilled by unchanging human nature; at first the dead animal swells and ripples but then gradually it flattens and becomes dust) a smile came to him as he thought of the joy which arises when one faces down a choice with repose and an "unnatural" response. The sublime orchestration and perfect visual satisfaction of the "dead rabbit" must concede an opposing analogy that could represent the wide-spread activation of another consistent "unnature" for no truly unnatural thing can exist in this world. There must be an unknown image, he thought, one that can represent this other possible fate.

Someone was knocking at the front door. He hesitated before answering since he habitually valued his invisibility. However, he'd decided at the outset that he wouldn't enforce his practice of sneaking around, he would open up and accept the woman's obviously permeable life. He clicked open the screen and faced a young green-eyed boy of about twenty-one.

"Is Carol here?" The boy asked.

"She's at work."

"At work? What the hell is that supposed to mean?"

"I don't know."

"Shit—at work, OK, sorry." The boy started to walk away. "Tell her that Denny knows she's out here."

He hadn't asked Carol much about her life. After looking around he had seen that the components weren't many. In any location to which a person adhered there were material limitations influencing imagination, and social limitations that did likewise; each person generally followed a fixed path which seemed natural but which was punctuated with just enough terror to feel alive. In the words Marx used to describe the aftermath to the June Insurrection of the Blanqui, "Following isolation, the proletariat becomes covert; ignoring societal change to focus on private salvation within its limited conditions of existence."

It is difficult to glimpse these lives without influencing them by one's presence. He recollected his many nights of drinking when, just before closing time, he would often attempt to latch onto any older woman who might have figured him for a student too drunk to notice age. Many times it worked out that he would be lured to the woman's apartment for more alcohol. He would have to play at avoiding sex without offending her; that is, he would have to appear to be too intoxicated to catch on to the drift of the conversation. With the functioning part of his brain he would observe the woman's behavior toward his own stupid and smugly grinning form attempting referential puns while knocking over a glass of cognac. The disassociation was always so complete that never once during one of these encounters did he make physical contact with a subject. The sun would eventually come up and he would leave.

These woman had wanted to use a poor boy (this characterization was the formula by which he justified his behavior); in exchange, he was allowed the chance to watch two strangers interact, even though one of the strangers would be he. For example, she had been: five feet, ten inches tall, brown hair in a short pixie cut flared with gel (it should have properly been standing upright but the utility of the style had passed so it had been tamed while she awaited the next breakthrough in modern hair), man's shirt, black jeans, expensive shoes of the sort worn by architects. She had a large rent-controlled apartment divided into only three rooms. They talked the usual bullshit together. She had insisted on cooking some catfish, he refused to eat it. The night pressed on and she talked about a friend of hers who had AIDS. This friend had apparently engaged in sexual activity with his lover while hooked to a ventilator in the hospital, dying two hours later.

At some point during the evening, another man had come into the apartment, disappearing into one of the other rooms. She explained, "That's my son." He thought that it would have been a good time to leave but he didn't want her to think it was because she had a son.

The sky had started to turn blue again when she leaned over to him and said, "Can you make it fit?" He hadn't known how this was meant to affect him so he mentioned that he wanted to run out and get some beer. He snapped himself (the viewer and the viewed) together and left the woman's apartment.

He still sometimes regretted not getting involved, taking his share of hurt and loss like everyone else. He figured he had certainly missed a chance to latch onto some rich woman but he just couldn't have gone out that way. He couldn't choose a side, could not proclaim (as he read in The Brumaire while remembering this period in his life), "property, family, religion, order."

It was dark in the apartment now but the heat had not subsided. Evenings here brought only the prospect of rain and a total cessation of breezes. Headlights glared through the screen door and he walked out front as Carol entered the apartment. She moved directly to her CD player and turned on some music. The persistent moisture of spring had deteriorated the connections on the machine so the hostile music she played was transmuted into a series of scratching noises with intermittent bursts of silence. Carol threw her purse across the room as though she had done it a thousand times. She crashed down into a bright red chair and crossed her arms over her chest. He waited for her to settle and then turned off the CD player.

"What's wrong? Was worked fucked up? Did you get fired?" He asked.

"No," she said.

"Some fool named Denny came by here looking for you."

"That figures. What did he say?"

"He seemed to be surprised that you were at work."

"I wasn't at work. I don't have a job."

"Where were you?"

"I went to get an abortion," she said. "Since I met you I've been trying to figure out how to get away from Denny, my boyfriend. He had the money and the place I used to live at. I thought if I slept with him one more time I could break up with him but he got me pregnant. I took the abortion pill the next day but I got drunk and he made me sleep with him again so it didn't take. At least I played it all out so I won but the pill didn't take and I had to go out today and get an abortion. I'd been going out looking for a job other days, just not today."

"Do you have AIDS or anything like that?" I asked.

"No fucking way. What kind of question is that?"

"It's just a lot of shit to hear. How come you didn't tell me earlier? Maybe I could have helped you or something."

"Why would you care? I didn't know how to tell you, it's just been nice hanging out with you. This wasn't your problem. I could handle it myself."

"It's still pretty disturbing."

"Why don't you leave then?"

"You must feel pretty sick. Maybe you should try and sleep. Did the doctor give you any instructions on how to recuperate? Did he give you any medicine?"

"No, he just sucked that thing out of me and killed it."

He searched through the contents of her purse scattered next to the wall and found a small envelope full of pills. Carol climbed into bed, took some of the pills and shut down, temporarily released from a sorrowful weight he couldn't understand and, luckily, would never be able to feel. As she slept, he returned to *The Brumaire* and finished his notes.

When he looked back at what he wrote that day, he was surprised to discover it steady, concise and perfectly representative of the events of that time. He hoped one day to shape for himself a final, authoritative draft. He had that right. It's a right we all share: to see things our own way.

If as Marx said (appending Hegel), "great personages appear in history twice, the first time as tragedy, the second as farce" then by finally traducing the needs entwined within that unfortunate spell in Iowa he could confront the reappearance of this spectacle any number of times, while always resolving the demonstration of desire as a form of madness to be isolated and subjugated. He believed the repetitive display of these events would finally reveal a method which could defeat the intimidation into needless and crippling self-recrimination which arises when contending with those forces that slowly envelop us from the first days of youth.

As soon as we feel, we feel ourselves owned, perhaps rightfully; we then remain brutally forgetful, exhausted and without the funds to bring about our own restoration, having never been adequately compensated for our initial, guiltless consent.

10

I REMEMBER CAR-TOONS

Across the street from Washington Irving Junior High School there stood a 7-11 store from which I would steal my extracurricular reading materials. In a month I might make three trips for the purpose of procuring humor magazines. During the first I'd grab the latest *Mad* and *National Lampoon*; on the second, *Crazy* and *Cracked*; if a third trip was needed, there at the end of the rack would sit my final quarry: *CARtoons*, the strangely beguiling yet highly technical humor magazine devoted to the absurdity inherent in America's obsession with the automobile.

Unlike *CARtoons'* core demographic, my interest in this magazine was strictly limited to satirical horsepower. I could no more relate to its baroque punch lines rendered in gap and torque than I could relate to the oblique references to clitoral stimulation on the jokes page of *Playboy* (the one with the mutant nymph sprawled inside the cocktail glass—and yes, I knew then what a cocktail glass was but that is a different story altogether). Despite this disjunction, I found the grotesque art inspiring and the exaggeration of vehicular monomania satisfying enough to last until the new issue of *Mad* came out.

As I grew older, *CARtoons* moved up on my theft list and increasingly touched an amorphous frenzy inside me that had yet to be named. *CARtoons* helped me to transcend the psycho-sexual violence and resentful confusion that swarmed through the life of an American teenager.

CARtoons is gone now and not much lamented. Perhaps endless variants on the melting engine joke proved replaceable over time, and yet, the tender element that the magazine crystallized in my soul stays with me and I find myself on the verge of paying homage to this humor magazine.

A Brief Publishing History

CARtoons was founded in 1959 by two guys, Pete Millar and Carl 'Unk' Kohler. It was published by Trends Books and later by Petersen Publishing. From the inception through 1979 the magazine's release schedule fluctuated from bimonthly, eight-a-year, quarterly, and back to bimonthly.

In 1964, the legendary "Unk and Them Varmints" were created. This brilliant synergy of fat street grease and exotic alien gremlins came to symbolize the possible epiphanies derived by conjoining elevated spiritual passion with automotive mechanics and finitely expressed all that *CARtoons* illuminated through its many and similar six-panel strips about four-engine ammonia-powered cars, much the way Alfred E. Neuman represented *Mad Magazine*.

In 1975, *CARtoons* hit its stride with a revamping and gained popularity in the wake of the "grotesque revival" that permeated the decade (i.e., Wacky Packs, Odd Rods, *Mad-Libs*, Slime, &c). It had a new logo, new artists, and new features, including custom iron-ons and a How-To section which led the reader step-by-step through drawing a certain car or truck. *CARtoons* began to destabilize again in the 80s. The iron-ons went out in July, 1983, returned in August, 1984, and then disappeared for good in April, 1986. They were replaced by color posters. Advertisements were also added at that time in a futile attempt to keep the cover price down.

In August, 1991, the last issue of *CARtoons* hit the stands. There was no warning of its demise, it was just gone. Subscriptions to *CARtoons* were changed to *Car Craft* for the remainder of the year and that was that.

At its peak, Petersen also published *Teen*, *CYCLEtoons*, *SURFtoons*, *Hot Rod CARtoons* and other magazines. The three other 'Toons books closed by 1974. In 1997, Petersen Publishing sued Time Inc. over the rights to the name 'Teen People' claiming it infringed on their mark 'Teen.' They lost this suit on appeal.

The Flying Eyeball

Just as Marvel Comics had "Nuff Said" and *Mad* its "Potrzebie" and "What Me Worry?", *CARtoons* had recurring wordmarks running subliminally through the magazine, sometimes scrawled in the margins or perhaps printed on a sign in the background of a random strip panel. The most important of these wordmarks was "Von Dutch" as in "Von Dutch is a dirty ol' myth" or "go-go-go Von Dutch." Von Dutch is the key to understanding the essence of *CARtoons'* application of graphic representation over the chassis of automotive passion.

Von Dutch was a man. Born Kenny Howard, Von Dutch was the primal car-striper and hot rod customizer. He hand-painted the outer skin of custom machines in painstaking, beautiful detail. When a car owner came to him, no one told Dutch what to do, just how much 'time' he wanted to purchase. The designs were up to Dutch. He had hundreds of imitators and followers: Shakey Jake, The Barris Brothers, Tweetie, Slimbo, Ed "Big Daddy" Roth, and others.

Von Dutch pioneered the ubiquitous 'Flying Eyeball' design. He lived the *Hot Rod* credo in its purest state, expressing his life through colorful decoration on over-stoked automobiles. Here is Von Dutch on the concept of money and the flying eyeball:

> "The flying eyeball originated with the Macedonian and Egyptian cultures about 5000 years ago. It was a symbol meaning 'the eye in the sky knows all and sees all.' I have always believed in reincarnation, and the eyeball was tied to that. I make a point of staying right at the edge of poverty. I don't have a pair of pants without a hole in them, and the only pair of boots I have are on my feet. I don't mess around with unnecessary stuff, so I don't need much money. I believe it's meant to be that way. There's a 'struggle' you have to go through, and if you make a lot of money it doesn't make the 'struggle' go away. It just makes it more complicated. If you keep poor, the struggle is simple."

The figure of Von Dutch is the archetype from which *CARtoons* evolved. *CARtoons* was a serial replication of the Von Dutch modus, an attempt to capture this form of spiritual devotion and reduce it to a linear display for legions of car fanatics. The humor magazine format effectively connected with readers seeking liberation through pictures of jet-engine-powered automobiles driven by a drooling Cyclops.

Content & Contributors

Like other humor magazines, *CARtoons* had a familiar stable of free-lancers who contributed to the magazine throughout its history. Some of the best-remembered contributors include George Trosley, Nelson Dewey and Rick Griffin.

George Troseley drew the "How-To" section and he created the long-running feature-strip "Krass and Bernie," about two dudes that lived in a one-car garage with a room above it. There was Bernie, the tall skinny guy, and Krass, his short sidekick. They were only into two things: cars and women. They could whip out a full custom car over-night, and still have time to go pick up some babes. "Krass and Bernie" was the first story in every issue, from February, 1975 to the last issue in August, 1991. Trosley also contributed to the *National Enquirer, Saturday Evening Post*, and *Hustler.*

Nelson Dewey contributed gag pieces from Issue #16 through the end. His style is instantly recognizable from his work in *Stunt Dawgs, Readers' Digest* and *Oui.* He specialized in human-relationship scenes set in cars or involving disputes over cars.

Rick Griffin is perhaps best known from his later career as a psychedelic illustrator, he designed posters in the Fillmore era and also designed album covers for Neil Young, The Grateful Dead, Jack Marshall, and The Challengers.

Other contributors of note include Willie Ito, who also drew "The Flintstones" and "Josie and the Pussycats," Shawn Kerri, whose cover drawing of the 'Haunted Hot Rod' is a classic, Renfrew Klang, George Lemmons, Jerry Barnett (later an editorial cartoonist for the *Indianapolis News*), Duane Bibby and Joe Borer.

Let's Look At Issue Number Twenty

The cover shows "Unk and Them Varmints" in a situation described thusly, "It's the night before Christmas and all around the Timing Stand them Varmints are waiting to decorate the Chrondek Tree that one lil' rowdy Varmint has just chopped down . . . to Unk's dismay."

"Dear Unk," the letters page, features sarcastic replies from the editor to hapless correspondents. For example:

> In my block everyone digs your magazine.
> We're waiting for someone to bury it.
> —*Dennis Olson, Austin, Texas*

> I didn't know you Texas-types could read.
> —*Unk*

A six-panel strip entitled "A-Doorable" is a variant on the theme of a large man emerging from a small car. A misunderstanding arises after an accident. One man rips away the door of the another man's car in anger and then he realizes that the man inside is huge and muscular. The smaller man is seen in the last panel with a welder, nervously reattaching the door he had previously ripped away from the car.

A four-page "Unk and Them Varmints" tale relates how "Them Varmints" dislike using public transportation but in order to satisfy Unk's demand that they "ride the bus" they buy a hot rodded bus that Unk can't resist. Featured in this strip are two other wordmarks used by *CARtoons*: "Hooray for Schmeerps" and "Moogaloonie!".

"Pink Slip Passenger" is a cautionary tale about a man who becomes exasperated by his date's backseat driving and gives her the wheel. She then precedes to race a carload of women she sees at a stoplight as the man hangs on helplessly. They get pulled over.

In "Stringin' Along" by Dale Hale, a man in a hot rod on his way to a hot rod show collides with a musical instrument delivery truck. Since the accident is clearly the fault of the deliveryman, and since the hot rod owner is running late for the show, they work out a deal. In the final panel we see the two standing side-by-side before the car which is adorned with a pair of harps replacing the front-grill damaged in the accident. The car has won first prize for "Most Original Grill." Both men are smiling.

Willie Ito and Carl Kohler render a tale set on the Bonneville Salt Flats in which visiting enthusiasts are preyed upon by an old man in a magnetically-powered hovercraft. A variant of the thieving-troll archetype, he comes out at night and steals car parts. He receives his comeuppance at the end of this seven-page story.

"Doctor's Orders" by Harry G. Harley relates the travails of a man prohibited by his doctor from driving his hot rod because he does not get enough exercise. His friend recommends that he drive a pedal-powered car instead. As he backs out of his driveway in a ridiculously small toy car, the under-exercised man happily exclaims, "Wheels is wheels!"

In a motorcycle jape entitled "Ram Jet," a man in a mountaintop race loses his bike but ends up winning by riding a mountain goat across the finish line. He revs up the ram by twisting its horns.

Rick Griffin delivers a four-page story about "Hapless Hank" who takes so long to build a custom Woody that by the time he finishes with it Woodies have gone out of style.

A quick six-panel gag, "Cool Duel," drawn by Jim Mueller, shows a man so short that he must be lifted up on a jack in order to challenge someone to a drag race. Scrawled on the grill of the short man's car, "Where's Von Fink?"

"Unsanctioned," by Jim Grube, tells the story of two friends who have an adventure at an unsanctioned drag strip featuring a dog as tech inspector, Fidel Castro as track official and Frankenstein's monster as security guard. The race is won by a bucktoothed villain in a stovepipe hat after he blows up his rival's car with a hand grenade.

In Closing

The back cover of issue twenty says it all, "Wanna Start Sumpin' Wild?" The caption refers to both the picture of a hand-cranked engine and the possibility of buying a subscription to *CARtoons*. In the sense that *CARtoons* magazine reflected, contained and evolved vehicular obsession through the grotesque I would say that it was a pretty good magazine, well worth stealing.

WHO is Von Dutch and WHERE is he? Even more important, WHAT'S an Unk Kohler and HOW did it get off Java Jetty? Gotta go now, I'm adjusting for skim on my slot-rod. It's Help Stomp on Varmints Week.

II

THE PASSIVE/AGGRESSIVE DYNAMIC

BETT: In any bet the risk must be high enough to sustain the anxiety the gambler feels at the prospect of losing. The stakes must be great in order to provide a palpable return so that victory justifies the waning of the anxiety. But when the game upon which the bets are riding becomes too predictable, or too chaotic, the competitive instinct, naturally, becomes displaced. The gambler's anxiety converges on the procedure and upon it exerts a reactionary sadism. The objective is no longer competition but rather the simulation of the competitive dynamic through the passive/aggressive embrace.

The common method by which corporate hegemony undermines the individual is to foster an atmosphere in which the passive-aggressive response and the impetus to sadism circumscribe choice.

For example, in this exchange from a magazine article about a lower-middle-class kid the dry tone of the questioning suggests a negotiation of propriety between members of two implacably fixed social classes:

> "Are you interested in girls?"
> "Yes." (He turns bright red.)
> "In girls you see on TV?"
> "Mostly in girls I know."
> "How do you like being twelve?"
> "I like it. I'm older. It's better than being eleven. You're taller. You can ride the go-karts at Snookers, out at Hickory Hollow Mall. At first when I got older and taller I didn't like not being able to play on bars at Chuck E. Cheese no more."

("Kid, Twelve" by Susan Sheehan, *The New Yorker Magazine*, Aug. 19, 1996)

The boy shifts into a second person description of himself. This marks the point at which the subject of the article begins to comply with the logic of the situation. He even goes so far as to point out specifically which Snookers he is considering. There is a conscious reversion to class allegiance by the use of "no more".

In a similar display of positioning, these readings from *The Wall Street Journal* note enchanting details of sensual proximity to the massif of corporate activity.

"The Dow 6000 champagne is getting warm."

"But while the rumor caused some knee-jerk buying of gold and silver futures it was quickly quashed by the State Department—"

"—Mr. Pestillo's uncanny track record for striking bold deals with the UAW and his golf-outings with Stephen P. Yokich, the UAW's sometimes prickly president."

(*The Wall Street Journal*, Sept. 5 and Oct. 10, 1996)

The alternation of luxurious imagery and class-defining strength is in the tradition of the passive/aggressive discourse. To partake of the fruits of this paradigm by capitulating to sadistic impulses creates an obligation to maintain and evangelize the passive/aggressive relationship. An antagonistic stance expressed towards an oppressor can only reaffirm the same necessary relationship, the subjugated have no opportunity to draw on historical models of rebellion without revealing a failure of the desire to compete within contemporary modes thereby mortifying themselves by a form of cowardice.

ORRWEL: The following chart appeared in *The Wall Street Journal*:

If Clinton wins:
HELPED: Apple Computer, Education Stocks, Financial Stocks, McDonald's, Tyson's Foods.
HURT: Drug Stocks, Textile Stocks, Tobacco Stocks, Toy Stocks.

If Dole wins:
HELPED: Correction Corp. of America, Defense Stocks, H&R
Block, Retailers, Security Stocks, Tobacco Stocks.
HURT: Bonds, Financial Stocks, Government Contractors.

("The Bill and Bob Portfolios," *The Wall Street Journal*, Aug. 21, 1996)

If one could discover the actual network of influences and effects connecting the incommensurate arenas of politics and the marketplace the relationship might appear more complex. The direct connection misinforms and taunts. Could a more causally explicative yet simplistic chart be printed? Why are simple information displays filled with simplistic information?

Corporate America is occult. In the wisdom of the spirit world, misdirection is endemic and explanations are judged strongest when they cannot be proven. We cannot attack, cannot seek to blunt, any form of incorporation by analysis for incorporation permeates ethereally.

Yip Harburg, author of both "Somewhere Over the Rainbow" and "Buddy, Can You Spare a Dime?", described the narrowing of range required in popular music when it sought to touch the superficial character of significant human yearnings:

"Cole Porter saw the world as an elite party, Hammerstein had a little more humanity. He felt for people. He was as corny as Kansas in August. Berlin saw the world as a hit song. Ira Gershwin saw the world as a smart song . . . Larry Hart saw songs as a means of stopping pretty girls from rejecting him. And me? 'It's only a paper moon, sailing over a cardboard sea, but it wouldn't be make-believe if you believed in me'."

("The Lemon Drop Kid" by John Lahr, *The New Yorker Magazine*, Sept. 30, 1996)

A workers' party could never have hoped to defeat organized management if America's true sentimental nature lent itself to optimism and expansiveness. Business was clearly a mechanism better suited for control than socialism. In this light, it seems amazing that any form of organized labor exists today. However, considering the gravitas of allegiance in the passive/aggressive economy, underwritten by the mystical effect of capital, "labor" retains its own noble sense of sentimental yearning and provides a distinctive arena for expressions of sadism.

It is always important to display information that affirms the possibility of an omniscient viewpoint. The dissonance between the desire to be individual and the desire to be within the community is a crucial neutralizing charm of the passive/aggressive dynamic. Statistics can be useful hexes.

> Opposition to affirmative action among white men surged to 67% in 1995 from 44% in 1991, according to a *Wall Street Journal*/NBC poll. But now that same anger has cooled a bit. According to the same poll conducted this year, opposition to affirmative action among white men has dropped to 52%.

> ("Mood Swing" by Jonathan Kaufman, *The Wall Street Journal*, Sept. 5, 1996)

The potential for advancement prevents the resolution of conflict. Every negotiation is useless in this sense because, although competition is actually a method by which standards can be raised, hierarchies contain competition as a closed and limited ritual honoring those who control the terms of engagement. Under these conditions, passivity can envelop the individual and cause them to drift until they are subsumed into some limited competitive dynamic over which they have some control. Alternately, all aggressive outbursts directed towards exclusion merely cause the individual to pull into the orbit of that aggression. Any direct and affirmative action becomes merely a form of expression which is wholly removed from the objective of the action. For example, rather than actually castrate the child molester, California seeks to euphemistically demonstrate its intention:

> California's new law permitting "chemical castration" of repeat child molesters has raised an array of ethical and constitutional issues. But some doctors and male patients now voluntarily

using the testosterone-lowering hormone say it also poses medical concerns—and may not even be effective when made compulsory . . . . Under a measure signed into law this week by California Gov. Pete Wilson, offenders convicted of repeatedly molesting children will be given weekly injections of the drug for the duration of their paroles.

("Will 'Chemical Castration' Really Work?" by Rhonda L. Rundle, *The Wall Street Journal,* Sept.19, 1996)

HJDO: In music, substance can be divorced from intention. Approached materially, music may be an element of the passive/aggressive dynamic, however, sound is unique for it can begin to exhibit the characteristic of language with only the slightest application of organizational pressures. This misapprehended sound is believed to signify but fails altogether to communicate. The action of music upon the individual can become a source of energy. Momentum may be created by this substance which travels through air disguised as language but is not adhered to any form of display. Responses may be discovered that are driven by this energy and which can rationally be denied to have been caused by the intentions of the organizers or sources of the sounds. Music might inspire action beyond capitulation to the mystical bases of incorporation and the passive/aggressive dynamic.

One last item closes this section (HJDO) with a specific example of human activity within the passive/aggressive order. The subject of this essay is action and this section concludes by contemplating action.

On July 30, a British jury acquitted four women of conspiracy and criminal vandalism for inflicting 1.5 million pounds worth of damage on a Hawk ZH955 fighter jet. The plane was bound for the Bandung squadron of the Indonesian Air Force. The first of twenty-four planes to be delivered under (a contract worth one billion dollars), it would have been used in General Suharto' war against East Timor. Since the Indonesian invasion of 1975, 200,000 people—a third of the population—have died in military assaults and forced settlement programs.

("Beat the Devil" by Alexander Cockburn, *The Nation,* Aug. 26, 1996)

The passive/aggressive dynamic merely adapts, absorbs and corrects in order to incorporate. The interchangeability of individualism and incorporation is inescapable. This is information that is both simply displayed and complex in its content.

12

DRACULA VERSUS
BILLY THE KID

No one riding the Fort Sumner stage that evening carried a mirror so no one could discover the identity of the dignified stranger sitting with them. Auntie Christian, her husband John P., and their solicitor did not know the man was Dracula. They spied on him discreetly as he dozed through the journey. His foreign manner of dress and his air of solitude led Aunt Christian to surmise the man was a judge or a railroad official. She could not understand why a man like this would be heading so far into the open country.

Where the trail passed Portales she could stand it no more. She leaned forward to address him, "Is the countryside boring to you?"

"Did I ask you to talk to me?" Dracula replied.

"I'm wondering what brings you out here. For instance, we happen to be traveling another day into the territory because my brother has died and left to me the operation of his ranch. These gentlemen ride with me," Auntie persisted.

"Ranching seems about right for a trio of fat fucking cows like you," Dracula mumbled.

"Listen, squanto, I don't know how they do things in whatever cocksucking club you got booted out of but around here the Christian family own just about everything so I'd show some manners before we decide to string you up." Auntie stood and pressed Dracula down into the bench with her strong, fat palm. "We worked hard to get what we got, you ass-lapping bumpoke. We have survived many winters' cold starvation with this bulk and we wear it proudly." Auntie raised her free hand and brandished a photograph of a young woman, "This is what comes from all that sacrifice. Feast your eyes on her beauty and grace."

Dracula studied the picture, "I'm assuming this isn't a picture of you before you forgot how to shit."

"Oh no, you delicate little bitch, this is my niece, Hillary. One day she will run this territory and do so with my family's blood running in her veins." The stagecoach lurched and Auntie stumbled with it. The photograph fell from her hand as the two gentlemen struggled to steady the woman. Dracula snatched up the picture and slipped it into his coat pocket.

They soon reached the inn at Portales. Dracula noticed a band of Apaches camped nearby. The men were drunk and entertaining themselves by tormenting a mule with hot sticks. A lone squaw sat aside, nearer to the trail. Dracula licked his lips.

"Don't mind those savages," the stagecoach driver said, "they're outcasts who trade with the inn. The warriors are on the road ahead. We should miss them if we rest here tonight."

Dracula slipped past the drunken Apaches and dragged the squaw off to a dry creek. He feasted on her blood and then assumed the shape of a bat to fly away.

In the morning, the stagecoach left the inn early with little concern for the whereabouts of the old stranger. The outcast Apaches discovered the dead body of the only woman they owned. They rode off after the stagecoach. They killed everyone aboard and grabbed what goods or cash they could carry.

After sunset, Dracula found the site of the massacre and switched the papers of John P. Christian with his own. Dracula set the stagecoach ablaze and tracked down one of its errant horses to ride in the direction of Fort Sumner.

Billy the Kid and Hillary Christian, the young lady in the photograph, were together near the Christian family ranch shooting at tin cans.

"Throw the cans straight this time or I might hit you with a shot," Billy demanded.

"Is it my fault you're shooting so poorly?"

"Toss them cans and shut up," Billy said.

Billy's hand twitched near his holster as Hillary launched the cans into the air. Billy sent them sailing with three quick shots.

Hillary grabbed the pistol from him. "It's my turn. Go grab the cans."

Billy did as she asked and was surprised when she hit two of them. "That's pretty lucky shooting," he said.

"I can work a gun."

"I guess I wouldn't marry a girl who couldn't."

That evening, Dracula arrived in Fort Sumner and made for Callahan's Saloon.

"I need a place to stay until the stage arrives tomorrow. My name is John P. Christian, I've come to town to take over the ranch."

"I thought you must have been someone," Callahan said.

"I have been riding a long time. Give me a key and I'll go up."

Dracula stepped on the leg of a drunk injun passed out near the back stairs. The injun opened his left eye and saw the image of a wolf skull on the man's shoulders. He grabbed at Dracula's cloak.

"Unhand me, savage. Let me pass," Dracula said.

"I know you, " the drunk injun mumbled.

"Black Mule! Let go of him, you old faggot—that's John P. Christian," Callahan shouted.

"The fuck he is," Black Mule said.

Billy the Kid came to Callahan's to get drunk and was warned that Mr. Christian had come to town on horseback, ahead of the stage. Billy went upstairs immediately to take the measure of his new boss.

"My name is William. I'm the foreman at the ranch. Do you want me to take you out there now?" Billy said to Dracula.

"I'm exhausted and I should wait for my wife; besides, I'm sure Hillary is in no mood to receive visitors. She must be terribly weakened by her recent tragedy." Dracula pulled the stolen photograph from his breast pocket. "Has she changed much since we were sent this picture? Is she still the jewel of the family?"

Billy started to make a joke about a cherry-red ruby and a pearl necklace but caught himself. Billy moved closer and spoke respectably, "She's as fresh and fine as the picture indicates. She has only grown stronger."

Dracula greedily swiped the picture out of sight and turned to face the young man. "That's why we came out here as soon as possible. She is the flowering of our family's toil and it isn't right that she should be burdened with such a responsibility. It is almost time for a young lady of her status to enter society and seek to make a profitable union."

Callahan stepped into the room and solemnly asked both men downstairs.

The saloon was full of noise. The sheriff shouted to the men mingling around him, "It was Apache. If you're sober and can handle a knife I'm giving a reward for their heads."

"What happened?" Billy asked.

"They found the old man's wife and the rest of the stage all dead," the sheriff said.

Dracula gasped in mock terror. He turned as if faint and ran up to his room.

"That's man is soft, Billy, you better watch out for him," Callahan said.

The next evening, Billy the Kid rode towards the main house of the Christian ranch. His work for the day was done and he thought he might take Hillary into town to check on the old man. Mr. Christian had been inconsolable, and he had not stirred from his room. Billy was therefore surprised to find him in the house, sitting on the couch with Hillary.

"Ware all that is left. I must put aside my own grief in order to set the business of this ranch aright and protect your fortune," Dracula said.

Hillary was staring into his eyes. She did not move as Dracula caressed her bare shoulder. Such was the scene Billy witnessed as he walked into the sitting room. Several minutes passed as he stood before the pair. All remained motionless as Dracula's stare penetrated Hillary's soul.

Billy spoke, "How are you getting along, sir? If there is anything I can do, let me know."

"Why is the help allowed to walk freely through the main house?" Dracula thundered.

Hillary shook her head rapidly. She pulled at her dress to cover her shoulder and said, "This is William. He's our foreman and a close friend to me."

"I'm aware of his rank; I'm simply asking why he is standing in the parlor tracking a rotten pair of shit-covered boots across my Persian carpet!" Dracula stood and wrapped his cloak around himself as an offense to Billy the Kid.

Billy could feel his blood rising at the abrupt strangeness of what he had seen.

"He is much aggrieved, William. I'll meet you tomorrow when we bring the new crew up from town," Hillary said as she led Billy to the door.

"Just make sure he isn't angry with me. If I fuck up I'll lose this job," Billy said.

"I'll talk to him." Hillary kissed Billy's cheek.

Obsessed by the sight of John P. caressing the shoulder of his niece, not one day after the death of his wife, Billy decided to drink a few in town.

"Who took John P. out to the ranch today, Callahan?" Billy asked.

"Maybe one of the sheriff's men."

"Did they cull any scalps?"

"I think they did the job. There was another body waiting for them in town, though. That old whore Polly got herself killed."

"That's too bad. I know we're all going to miss her," Billy said.

The drunk injun Black Mule yelled out, "There's going to be a lot of missing to be done before long. It was me that found Polly. I was out looking to bust one before they brought those Apache heads back. Alas, I remain unsatisfied and have had to double up on this piss you sell as whiskey. I'm not one to defile the dead, although that would have been a better fate than what awaits Polly now."

"That syph has eaten your brain," Billy said.

"I saw her. Her throat was stabbed but there wasn't a drop of blood anywhere. Now, if you'll forgive me. I must sleep," Black Mule said.

"Too scared to drink, now?" Billy asked.

"I'm going up to your ranch on the new crew tomorrow. I figure I should lay in some silver before this town goes bust. I'll have to move on soon, I'm sure of it." Black Mule dragged himself out to the street.

Billy the Kid downed another shot as the saloon doors banged still. "Black Mule might be right about one thing: if the ranch doesn't get back to where it was this town will be finished."

"You'll get it together. You've got plenty of reasons to stick it out. You have really changed your tune, Kid. I'm proud of you, " Callahan said.

"I hope it's worth it. The straight life hardly ever pays off, " Billy said.

"You missed breakfast, Uncle." Hillary stepped carefully as she entered the study where Dracula was poring over the accounts. "It's so dark in here."

"The dim light aids my concentration," Dracula said. "These ledgers are in terrible shape. I assume the foreman had a hand in that."

"God has given us this chance to set aside our sorrow and put our hearts right with some hard work," Hillary responded hopefully. "Although these recent tragedies are never far from my mind I somehow feel invested with strength when I think of building this place up once again. I feel our lost family members working through my hands. You, me and William; we're all that's left."

"You should be running along," Dracula said.

"I'm going to see how the new crew are doing. Would you like to go out with me and get some fresh air?" Hillary asked.

"I'll be here all day," Dracula said. "I have work at hand." He tilted his head slightly to watch Hillary's thighs brush together as she left the room.

That night as Hillary slept Dracula visited her bedroom. He drank a small taste of her blood. Frenzied with lust he flew off to satisfy himself on the cattle.

Billy discovered the slaughter when he rode the morning inspection. He dragged the carcasses down to save what he could and went to the main house to report the killing.

"Mr. Christian, there was some trouble with the herd last night," Billy said.

"Close that curtain, boy!" Dracula shouted.

"Some head were attacked and killed. I brought the remains in."

"You can't just dispose of beef without asking me."

"I didn't want to waste it," Billy said.

"You do nothing without my approval. The next time this happens it could mean your job, you insolent fool," Dracula sneered. "And furthermore, I'm not going to allow Hillary to continue fornicating with the likes of you. Her sexual initiation needs be handled delicately, by a man with experience—not fumbled through by some inbred and mentally defective teenage outlaw."

Billy felt his hands move to his guns. He stopped and thought of the trouble it would bring. He backed away, stumbling on the carpet.

"You're getting weak, Billy." Dracula said.

Billy lifted himself from the floor without looking at the old man. His knee had been gashed by the foyer steps and so he limped out to his horse.

A few days passed while Billy the Kid waited for something to come of the confrontation with John P. Chirstian but it only simmered.

In that time, Hillary had taken to her uncle with a feisty loyalty. Today she would be escorting him up to the mines at the back of the property. Operations there had been abandoned years before. Technical innovations had developed since and Uncle John had Hillary convinced that the hills might yield anew some valuable metals.

Billy visited Black Mule. His knee still ached and he hoped to get some of the old man's medicine or maybe even some morphine to hide his pain. Black Mule dug an old book from his satchel and handed it to Billy.

"I can't read, Mule, you know that," Billy said.

"This book shows things. Look at the pictures and see if any remind you of Mr. Christian."

"I don't know," Billy said. "All those eastern fellows are pale."

"Do the Christians have any mirrors up in the house?"

"There was a mirror in the front room but I don't recall seeing it last I was there. I think it was sold to bring down some of the debts. Hillary loved that thing but she goes along with what he says."

Black Mule took the volume from Billy and explained, "This book talks about a kind of man that lives in a different way than most. We've both seen a lot of killing but can you imagine a man that feeds on the men he kills?"

"I heard they had some injuns like that down on the gulf coast," Billy said.

"This book isn't about injuns. It's about a kind of man who lives by drinking the blood of other creatures."

"What are you trying to do to me? Don't I have enough trouble already?"

"There's been five more head killed and the whore Polly. I saw her and it was just the way this book describes it. A man who lives this way would think nothing of taking his own niece."

"Did you see him messing with Hillary, too?" Billy stammered.

"These blood men have a certain power to them. They slowly drink of the blood of young girls, each time bringing the girl to the threshold of the great journey. Soon the girls sicken and die but arise on the next night as slaved creatures forever bound to the blood men," Black Mule said.

"No one can live forever," Billy said.

Hillary pulled back on the reins and stopped at the mouth of the old mine cut into Lexington Hill. Dracula surveyed the area in the twilight and found it suitable.

"We could have made it here faster if I'd taken the front road," Hillary said.

"I prefer the shade of the hills, my dear." Dracula turned to her and touched her hand. "You're such an impetuous girl. I hope my stabilizing influence will help you to grow more mature." Hillary fell into a shallow sleep under Dracula's gaze. "We have not much time before we can be together, you beautiful thing. After I make you my slave we shall rule The West together from atop this very hill. I believe that when I make my mark tonight I will taste the soft flesh of your thigh. Don't you long for the life I offer?" Dracula whispered.

"I want it." Hillary's voice was unreachably deep and mechanical.

"I could tell from the photograph you were a girl awaiting adventure,

trapped out here in this ridiculous life surrounded by ignorant beasts."
Dracula broke his hold on her. His powerful senses had detected a
horse galloping towards them. He lifted a coffin out of the carriage
bed and slipped inside the mine just as Billy the Kid rode up.

"Hillary!" Billy slapped her face. She weaved a little as though she
were faint and then began to blink her eyes rapidly.

"Where's Uncle John?" Hillary shook her shoulders.

"Are you all right?" Billy asked.

"I'm just tired, baby. I don't feel well." Hillary smoothed her skirt
distractedly.

"Shit, you ain't pregnant are you?"

"No, Billy, you can't get that way from swallowing it," Hillary
explained.

"How long have you been sleeping out here?" Billy asked.

"For a while. We came up to inspect the mine. Uncle John has such
grand plans for us."

Billy banged his saddle, "Ever since he came here all I've been hearing is how great that old dyke is; but things have been going nothing
but wrong. I don't trust that reptile. I don't like the way he looks at you
and the things he says about you."

"William Bonney! I'm ashamed that you would be jealous," Hillary
fumed.

"Back east it don't make no difference to those rich turds, they like
to keep the punny in the family. There's something wrong about him.
Why'd he go and leave you all alone when it's getting dark? There's
something prowling around killing cattle."

Dracula emerged from the cave.

"Fuck that old rat," Billy said. He slapped his mount and headed off
towards Callahan's Saloon.

"What did that imbecile want?" Dracula asked as he climbed
aboard the carriage.

"He's upset about all the cattle getting killed." Hillary snapped the
horses forward.

"Indeed," Dracula said. "Ask William to come and see me tomorrow.
I need to talk with that boy."

The next day, Billy the Kid limped into Dracula's darkened study. He felt so low and drunk he didn't talk. He hung his head as he sat down.

"I've been receiving reports that you have been undermining my authority with the hands," Dracula said. "Beside the recent plague of dead cattle, which you have failed to stem, I have also some questions about your former occupation that I would like answered. If I am to correct the dreadful state of this concern I must have solid, trustworthy men on board. If I fail in this endeavor the town and the territory will suffer greatly. Is it possible to rest such a burden on the shoulders of a man like you?"

"What the fuck do you know?" Billy muttered.

"I know I'm the man who owns you. You might have deceived my brother-in-law and preyed upon their daughter but I am forged from stronger stuff."

"I think it's pretty strange the way you ride into town, this cat no one has ever seen before, and they just turn the ranch over to you. I think it's unlikely you'd be able to go a full day's ride by yourself through Apache country."

"They saw what was left of the stage. The sheriff confirmed it," Dracula said.

Hillary entered the room carrying a hand mirror.

"Come in, Sugar, your boy is getting the boot," Billy said.

Hillary stepped forward and Billy caught a glimpse of an empty leather chair as the mirror reflected the far side of the room.

Dracula stopped Hillary before she could advance. "Did I not ask you to remove those objects of vanity from this house?" Dracula demanded as held Hillary firmly.

"You asked me to fix my hair," Hillary said.

"Please leave us," Dracula said implacably.

"Tell her how you got me on the hook for everything that's gone wrong around here," Billy said.

"I have decided that William is not capable of handling his duties. He'll be leaving today," Dracula said.

"But we were going to be married," Hillary said.

"I am your legal guardian and I don't want you near this man. A girl's interest in outlaws and toughs must give way to the propriety her station demands." Dracula easily pushed Hillary out of the room. He slammed the heavy door. Billy heard her faint sobs and objections fade behind it.

"You have hurt her tender mind but that is your nature," Dracula said. "You will be escorted from the property. If you return, the sheriff has orders to arrest you."

Billy the Kid stayed drunk at Callahan's for the next few days. He slept on the piano rather than paying for a room. The failure of his plan to lead a straight life had left him with but his true talent for killing intact; it came to him that he should ride back to the ranch and use that talent to its fullest extent. He stopped at Black Mule's cabin to see if he might wish to join up and ride. Billy explained all that had transpired.

"I was right. The mirror proves it," Black Mule said.

"Not a fuck we can do except shoot him. No one will believe my story, now," Billy said.

"It also says in the book he must sleep inside a coffin hidden deep and cool."

"I saw him up at the old mine with Hillary."

"The book says we must track him there and drive a stake of wood through his immortal heart," Black Mule said.

"These should work fine." Billy tapped his six-shooters.

"No, he must be staked, and the girl rescued or be damned."

"She turned on me, fuck her. I've been in town. Where's she been?"

"Those are cowards words, Billy. You have a chance to stand and fight for something worth the trouble."

Billy the Kid knew the code of his desperado past: it was worth any risk to make a big score. Maybe he was about to take his biggest haul ever, and all he had to do was be himself and kill.

Dracula slipped into Hillary's room again that night. He had been careful not to drink too deeply, she could not die yet. Over the last week he'd slowly brought her to the climax he'd longed to reach. After this extraction of blood she would be ready.

Dracula flew away above the ranch to seek out a creature upon which to feed. Even as he crafted his domination of the girl he had still to attend to his own thirst and nourishment.

In spite of the intrusions he'd been tolerating Dracula nurtured the sensation of relief he would soon know while defiling Hillary for what would be the first of the many times he would take her until he grew bored. It always became boring. For now, the thrill of the hunt raged inside him and it made that inevitable result seem tantalizingly distant.

Billy stalked past the windows of the main house searching for Mr. Christian.

From the darkness the sheriff called out, "Drop it, Kid. I know you might think this will fix everything but you've been drinking an awful lot. Come in with us and sleep it off, we'll straighten everything out tomorrow."

"He's been killing her, and taking her womanhood. I have to finish him off and get what's mine," Billy said.

"I've been easy on you, Billy, but this is the end. I barely believe you can stand there and talk, as drunk as you must be." The sheriff and his deputies laughed at this.

Dracula emerged from behind a stand of mesquite. Billy raised his gun. The deputies tackled him and slapped on the irons before Billy got a shot.

"This is a town where the rule of law is strong. We won't bow to your kind," Dracula said.

"He and Black Mule must have been up at the bunkhouse raising hell. Billy must have got lead up his ass and thought to come see you and the girl. Were you hit, sir?" The sheriff asked.

The sheriff packed Billy the Kid up on his horse and led it away.

Billy reclined in his cell watching the sheriff throw one-cent coins at a hat across the room. He knew he could pull his skinny legs and arms out of the irons but he couldn't get past the cell bars. If he hadn't been so drunk and tired he might have got a shot off back at the main house. Black Mule had said it wouldn't do any good but it had never failed before.

Suddenly, Black Mule stumbled into the jail and collapsed to the floor. "I got kicked off the ranch. Give me a room," he said.

The sheriff knelt down. A thin thread of tobacco juice dangled from his lips. He tried to lift the injun.

"You spit on me," Black Mule slurred. He snatched the sheriff's pistol and threw it past the bars to Billy.

"It seems crazy now but I have to go back. You'll understand when it is over. Give me the keys," Billy said.

"You will hang for this," the sheriff said.

Billy pushed the sheriff into the cell, "Let's go, Black Mule, there's still time to get up to the mine."

"I just walked all the way here, man. I'm tired. Lock me in this cell where it's safe," Black Mule said.

Billy grabbed a fast horse and headed out as the first streaks of dawn rose over the scrub.

Crouching beside his coffin within the depths of the old mine, Dracula was irritated by the consternation of the twisted route he had been forced to navigate. Had his contempt for the old woman on the stagecoach not coincided with that delectable feminine vision thrust in his face this confluence of circumstance might have eluded him and he would have been in San Francisco as planned. The city was a refuge for both exotic and common races; a banquet of indulgence and oblivion he would have been free to sample were he not entangled in this rustic comic opera.

"I defer the final strike. I put obstacles in my own path. I place myself at the center of an aggravating maze in order to heighten the sensuality of my inviolate course. I judge it a fair thing to handle myself this way since I'm damned to stalk the human race until the earth stops spinning. I provide a challenge for them. I inspire them and I keep myself entertained. However, the natural correction of predator and prey is eternal and so, Hillary, you should count yourself among the lucky few never forced to contemplate the aftermath of my appearances in time. I grant this gift sparingly and I grant it to you." Dracula hovered over Hillary's body. He pushed back her hair but then paused. "Let us have one more incident before I have the girl. This outlaw inspires more frustration than I have felt in years."

Billy the Kid stumbled noisily into the lair. Dracula glided towards Billy and threw him off balance. Billy embraced him.

"I'll hold on until you bring me close to that coffin. I'll kill her myself," Billy said.

Hillary was stirred from her slumber when the pair crashed into a row of pickaxes hanging from the wooden braces lining the cave.

"I can kill with your own gun as easily as I might rip open your throat. That would be an ignoble way for a legend to die," Dracula said.

Billy let his knees give out. They stumbled together in the dirt and Billy's gun skidded towards the coffin.

Bullets bounced around them as they struggled prone. Hillary was awake. A spike of tattered wood now dangled from above, splintered by Hillary's gunplay. The vampire saw the stake descend to pierce his breast. He let out a tired sigh as his heart was punctured. His body decayed rapidly but Billy still held him close in case Black Mule's remedy proved false.

"That's pretty lucky shooting," Billy said.

Billy the Kid was exonerated although the official record never matched the truth in detail. With Hillary standing witness, it was established that the man she took to be her uncle had preyed upon her unnaturally and would have succeeded in that as well as grand larceny and impersonation had not Billy the Kid stood up to him. Hillary and William married and the ranch thrived considerably. Black Mule was installed as foreman and Chaplin.

Although he'd left his outlaw days behind, Billy was still a wanted man. From time to time someone would come to Fort Sumner on a tip but with local help they'd get set wrong and move on. The town depended on Billy the Kid.

In order to finally erase his past, Billy contrived that he be gunned down publicly in a faked assassination. It is commonly held that he was at last killed and buried in the Fort Sumner Military Cemetery in New Mexico.

The true provenance of the bones within that grave have been a matter of public dispute over the years. Scientists in our own time have requested exhumation, a request that the loyal Fort Sumner descendents have consistently denied. It is understood among the natives that buried beneath the monument to the legend, behind the chain link fence erected to keep out the curious, are the remains of something far more disconcerting than a hollow western myth. If they were to open the grave they would find a set of bones mingling those of a sharp-fanged wolf and a man of about six-hundred years at the time of his death.

13

THOSE ARE JUST STORIES

Eddie Retanan faced the door of the Cai recording studio. He paused on the steps, a timid child. He watched as the people in the alley dragged themselves along through the low morning smoke. A man leading a badger on a leash hurried past. It trailed a clinging, musky wake. Eddie kicked the scuff plate on the glass door of the studio and entered the air-conditioned sanctuary.

Eddie had needed to piss since leaving home but there was no time for that. This was his first chance in a session at the island's top studio. It was a session with one of the biggest stars in the country. He guessed that holding a piss this long probably put a pained look on his face which might make him seem sexy. Three people looked him over as he walked in and he was sure the receptionist kept her eyes on him much longer than the two men perched before the mixing console who turned away quickly and continued their conversation.

"I got two songs about the mother. One with the ghostly hands of the mother stroking her face in a dream. That'll go into the movie. In the other she asks her mama about love—it mentions going to bed, but it's sweet."

"She's almost fifteen, now."

"That electric organ came in from the states so I want to feature it. We got the only one on the island."

"Kid, can you work this thing?" They both looked at Eddie. He stalked to the keyboard and spread his fingers across it.

"I can," Eddie answered.

"Donny told me you were good. You're lucky he likes to fight—how's he going to play with only seven fingers?"

The receptionist served tea. Eddie ignored her. He stared at the music machine. He stroked the frail hair on his face. He'd been trying to grow a beard for two weeks ever since he saw Kenny Rogers and The First Edition perform on TV.

One of the producers stood up, the one with gold plastic glasses. "When's the little girl going to get here?"

"She was out all night. Mama's bringing her in. We need to get this together before she shows up. I don't want any shit from that bone-dry bitch."

While the band rehearsed the tunes, Eddie noticed that the men in the booth had moved from their seats. While no boss watched, the drummer started up some fast time. Eddie let his right hand wander around the keys. He started getting that feeling where he fell away into a vast calm.

"Quiet! Stop that jerk-off shit." Gold Plastic had returned. Behind him in the booth stood Lia Cuneta and her mother. It seemed to Eddie that her mother wore all of the gold Lia might have earned. The mother was arguing with the producer and her long, long fingernails snagged on her own sheer scarf as she rapped his chest. The yelling trailed off and Lia left the booth as her mother tended to a broken nail. Lia's fingernails were painted pink to match the color of the child's dress she wore. Her black glasses blunted any expression from her face and probably hid beautiful, bloodshot eyes. She looked so scrubbed and clean.

"Move it. She stands there," Lia's mother yelled as the star took her place at the microphone. The singer faced Eddie. Lia removed her glasses and Eddie saw her eyes at last. Her eyes were red but Lia smelled nice.

"Get it right. Bring it down for a solo and give me at least five different voices from that organ, kid. That's our sound," Gold Plastic said. "Once or twice, that's all the time we have—the girl is very busy today."

Lia cleared her throat as the pedal steel player started the song. She began to sing:

I begged you for years to be stronger
Only a real man can survive in this world
But you always held your temper and forgave me
And I felt myself fading away.

I tried to make you angry
Your friends told you that I was bad.
But all I ever wanted was a man beside me
I wanted you, but you were so weak.
And then last night you found me
In the arms of another man
You won my heart again
When you shot him
And became the one I always wished you to be.
But now my heart is locked up with you in prison.
Until we can be together once again.

Eddie pumped his right foot down on the volume pedal of the organ and took his solo. As he popped the keys and worked the switches of the modern organ's electronics the other musicians stared at him with surprise but never lost the tempo. He glanced up when he had finished and saw Gold Plastic nodding in the booth. Eddie was young but he had studied hard for this chance. Lia sang another verse and chorus. The track was done.

There was a pause, a hush and the buzz of amplifiers.

"That's the one. You can clear out."

Eddie heard Lia mumbling something in Spanish but he couldn't understand. She walked over to him and leaned on his chair.

"You're new here. What is this thing?"

"It's a Lowry electronic organ. They just got it."

"You play very well," Lia said.

Eddie realized everyone was leaving the room and he knew the pissful clench he'd been holding for three hours could now be relieved in triumph.

"I have to go, they said to clear out."

"Bye." Lia waved to him as he left.

As much as he wanted to stand there like the ace he was and be drawn into Lia's world, his gut throbbed from throttling back the pressure he'd been feeling all day. It was one good thing for his balls to be throbbing but not for this reason—better from the rattling of the drums or Lia's body.

He wandered down the hall to find the washroom and he started to daydream, imagining his face painted on a billboard facing the U.S. Army base. The receptionist grabbed him by the arm rudely, as if she had caught him stealing.

"Where do we send the check?" She asked.

"I can't use a check. I need cash." Eddie had planned for this. He was not going to give out his address, they'd know what part of town he lived in; it would be better of they thought he lived on the street or in the bars and clubs.

"All right. Three days from now you have to come back for another track—I'll give you the money then."

Another session meant that Eddie had stolen the keyboard job like he knew he could. He stood there in the hallway, dazed. Suddenly, Lia was standing next to him and this was no daydream. She touched his arm and watched over her shoulder through the glass window of the control room as her mother ranted at a police officer.

"They want me to sing at the President's birthday celebration," Lia said quickly while she watched her mother.

"The President?"

"That's what I say. I'm going to Disco Havana to see HotDog tonight. Want to meet me there?"

"Nothing could stop me," Eddie said.

"Be out front at around ten. I'll get you in." Lia smiled but pulled away from Eddie's side as her mother and Gold Plastic came down the hallway.

They escorted Lia back to the studio. The police officer started clearing people out and Eddie was suddenly no one and he got ejected himself. It didn't matter, unlike the magazine writer or the movie theater agent or the fans who had infiltrated the crowd in the lobby Eddie would be back in a couple days; he would be back here to work.

Out in the street he realized he had missed his chance to piss. He went into the alley he had passed through on his way here this morning. At first he thought he was alone but someone stood up and moved out from behind the bales of trash along the wall. It was Donny, the old piano player who had given him this job. Donny looked sick, the bandage on his hand was soaked dark red and yellow.

"Hello, little guy, I see you're done working."

"You don't look so good," Eddie said.

"I was trying to sleep back here until you finished."

"I'm all done." Eddie looked past him down the alley.

"I bet you did fine."

"I did."

"I need my half of the money now," Donny said.

"Your hand looks worse. You won't be able to work for a while," Eddie pointed out.

"That's why I'm glad you did so well. You can fill in for me until I get better and pay me half each time. I'm sure you're glad I could give you this shot. We can really help each other. Music is the place for people like us. We have no luck, only the sharing that we can take upon ourselves. We have soul, not like those rats with the money. Do you want to come with me and have a drink together? You can tell me more about Mel Tillis and Jimmy Smith. When I get better we should make a plan to go to Hawaii, to play in the Hilton there. That's where we should be, little guy. Do you have that money? I'm starting to feel pretty weak." Donny extended his bandaged fist.

Eddie noticed a metal bar leaning against the alley wall. He grabbed it and with both hands slammed it across Donny's face. As Donny fell, his wounded arm drove straight down like a spike and the abscess ruptured. The smell enraged Eddie. While he pounded the fallen man Eddie remembered the pressing need he had been ignoring all day. He threw the metal bar down and unbuttoned his pants. He splashed Donny's body with a whip of urine that took many minutes to unload.

"The job is all mine and so is the money." Eddie fixed his pants and left the alley heading towards the nightclub district.

14

RODEO MATTRESS

The rodeo mattress was a mattress I found on the street in Washington, DC. The year was glorious 1985. The rodeo mattress had been thrown out to the curb with the entire contents of a vacant building. It was a child's mattress patterned with brown and yellow images of rodeo riders, steer ropers and broncs.

A homeless man was sitting near the pile. He was writing on a discarded stream of computer output, the old green and white paper perforated at every fold. I bought that accordion of scribble for three dollars. I've been reading it ever since and I will keep it around.

Many people criticize and dismiss personal languages as obscure or solipsistic and I agree with that sort of criticism when there is symbolic intent, when it is coded or concealing, dishonest. In this instance I have fortunate proof of good authorial faith. Knowing the source as I did and having seen the very same limited section of the city described in the work I could trust it enough to immerse myself. The subjects are verifiable, the text is not coercive or revelatory as so much personal language usually is; the style and impenetrability do not connote a fraudulent mystery. Detachment from the influence of meaning allows the pure effort to demonstrate a useful process of harmonically relating ideas to descriptions of material subjects.

> 1985, REAL ESTATE DEVELOPER: spit in his palm, spit shine, slaps the cowlick down, warbles with wit. His seed falls, does not catch at the crook in the roots. His seed rolls into the sewer. Butt licked clean, he gets pushed through the Department of Urban Renewal on a hand truck, papers are slapped into his hands. Lost one of his diminished bride's daughters to an 'OK guy,' a tripe cooked down

thick as winter stew. He scratches his elbow. The fingernails are too long and chafe him. He hires upstate relatives and brings them to town. They have evolved by race mixing with sick bear over many years. They help guard the other daughter who sits propped open in an ornate chair. The back of the chair is decorated with a red circle in the center of a scratched gilt frame surrounding a series of three paper birds, in progressively lighter colors, labeled 'noon spin-off,' 'rodeo mattress,' and 'memorial to Gilbert White.'

Turnout up, going to tell you about, had mean—, I said had mean—, the right. The mailman brought the wrong package. Voice in the key of 'no.' The packages were mislabeled and we had to pay for them, for children inside we then look. It's a silly stop to the mailman. I told them there was a child in the box that can't no tide damage.

The Statue of Liberty and hot dogs, Hitler Vurst, grass and water. The king had a thing, thought he was glass, so crazy from screwing each other. King and Queen were sister and brother. The King is made of glass, let's have a blast. Swermany, Itzerly, hollow milk-white eyes looking for obedience. Redneck Paradise: the revival of an old ordinance about Coney Island. A confusion of tongues. They talk American. Plums as big as apples. A game for players still to play.

SUBJECT #16 ST. ELIZ.

THURSDAY 13:00:17. It is done. Her bullshit is chilling but it took me all of ten minutes to get down. Hypnotism is for dunces but it works. Had remarkably few intrusive fantasies.

FRIDAY 15:00:27. Yesterday I balled the night nurse. It took about three minutes to get down and debauch. Today I focused on some cosmetic modifications. Decided to change filter for box shots from pink to amber. Threw up some lampreys I had eaten before my evening session. Cleaned up the mess. Session was stopped before things got violent. They need to streamline the procedure.

TUESDAY 09:42:01. The nurse came back from her vacation and was completely satisfied. Still to do: drag and strap, vulva battery, hide valves, turn on the circuit and shock someone; small modifications. Most unnoticed: 'hidden' penis, optional hiding of furs, multiples of the 'folksy' argument.

LINK TO NATIVE SEED INFORMATION: A reprinted etching set lopsided above a temperance caption. Ash, spit, passing fists, sailor flexing, many roomed mensch, pony expressway horse rape, a sparkling equine eye in the dust at Bull Run. I was looking through my mail in the lobby of The Parker House. I noticed you in the lobby. You were as static as a poster: caked and painted brow, every other shoe-step framed in black.

My family can trace its roots back to the 11th century. We lived in Northern Italy near the French border. One of the earliest tales in our family involves the Black Death. So numerous were the dying that not all could he given their last rites in time. This meant they went to hell. Therefore, sensing an opportunity, my ancestor worked the country-side posing as a peripatetic priest who would be prevailed upon to perform last rites in exchange for cash donations. With the fortune he made before Pope Clement's edict of 1348 (which stated that death by plague was an automatic remission of all sins) our family moved to France and bought into a shipping company.

Can't hurt someone who is dead inside, that's the scrape, my friends. It was so fun when we went back and watched ourselves, lost track of time. The seasons flattened, the flies took refuge. I caught a glimpse of someone young and aglow, less beautiful than the swollen asphalt below.

TOP FLOOR SUITE NUMBER: It's a saying: 'This island is all cleaned dirt.' We agree: everywhere in the world of deeds, these quarters can't be outdone. We don't know if it will hold out until HE can shine right but whom we most believe blind will take over. Many keep asleep and make all good works pay. Why would you move and get burnt black your hand? It doesn't fully explain the intense quiet. Bound, expelled to sleep around noon after packing my bags. I'm leaning up against you Linda to take our union like the thrashing of cattle through a gate. You pass through their courts and you do whatever they want you to do. We stand together like grain before the wrecking ball, we're mixed up. Yellow of raw, juvenile strutting meat spraycan'd 'Disco Dan' on the wall. I don't believe he was tried as a juvenile for it was not he that backed out. I said his room, yes, mine is number 945. You get a twenty and soon you're broke. I'm all sensation and all that wrecked around like cash. The man in the top floor suite, hacking, said: 'I will drops the hammer!' Amen to that.

WEERKAT AT THE DOCKS: Part Twelve, City Officers Plant 50 Ks of StereoJake Weed.

WeerKat mumbled tiredly at his cheap telephone. He hated his tenants, especially the college wrestler who proved to be far 'kattier' than he. WeerKat's ordeal could be ended. He needed only to line up some replacements. He would choose his new tenants from among the people who led the old Medicare patients through the park. When one is playing to the gallery in terms of living space, a job is the first thing at which one looks.

WeerKat handed over his tenants to the cops for lilacs and books, the arid crack of betrayal echoed through the house. WeerKat watched them double time the squatters like relics, pearls. They all came screaming down the stairs and scattered to the yard. The wrestler hopped over a wall but couldn't get past the security door.

'Good deal, why let them riot when they could provide reliable information to the Police and klux everything up?' WeerKat asked himself. 'I'm quite sure that once they're arrested they'll be beaten.'

I dragged my rodeo mattress home and sat down on it. I read my newly acquired volume of lore like a bent agent of the General Accounting Office going over fantasy budget estimates for ass-kickings projected to be delivered over a ten-year period. Some friends came by my place and I showed off my score. I was bested, however, as they had discovered a vacant building yet filled with storage owned by an old lady for whom they had done some yard work. In a quick strike they had lifted about twelve rolls of silver dollars. We drank pretty well for a few days. I hit the house by myself and I came out with two watches to sell and some more silver dollars. I remember being drunk, a few months later, when I sold the address to a congressional intern for a glass of something yellow, probably rum with no ice.

15

INTERSTELLAR TACO STAND

Seven men wearing identical suits filed along the gravel path leading to Taco World's suburban corporate headquarters. They disappeared through the lobby door. Gone for a moment, they emerged into the right wing of the single storey building, visible through the wall-length windows. As they gathered around a conference table one man, the boss, broke away. The scene inside was concealed when he drew down the blinds. The dark windows reflected the rainy sky above.

In the research department, Marty Cobbins had fallen asleep. The junior chemist faced a crucial deadline yet he had given way to exhaustion. He was slumped on the white counter, head and arms flat amid a proliferation of scientific instruments. His body was being supported by a tall chair that crept away from the counter on its small chrome rollers as Marty drifted through a beautiful dream.

Marty was sitting on the set of a talk show. He was far from the host, a sexy starlet sat closest to the host. She laughed explosively. The host leaned across the desk and asked, "Can I borrow some of your Nobel-prize-winning mind control serum? This woman won't stop laughing." Marty smirked and shrugged as the sexy starlet fell across his shoulder. The audience applauded and howled with greater and greater intensity.

Marty awakened from his dream. The chair had rolled far away from the counter where he had perched his head. Marty fell to the floor pulling metal and glass implements down with him.

The skies cleared and the next day dawned warm and bright. Lynn Henderson was eating lunch at the taco stand near her office. She was sitting on a plastic bench outside in the sunlight. Her feet were spread open and she leaned over gingerly so as not to drip the dark hot sauce on her stylish white pants. As she ate, a red stain started to spread from the inside of the crotch of her pants. When she had finished lunch and stood up to leave, the stain had widened obtrusively.

Marty was sitting in a fancy restaurant nearby. He was having lunch with his mother and stepfather. They had been waiting for almost an hour for the waiter to take their order. They'd had some drinks.

"Did you get that bruise wacking yourself off?" Marty's stepfather asked, pointing to Marty's face.

"It's work related." Marty touched his blackened eye.

"Slow down on the—" Marty's mother tapped the wineglass sitting before her while staring at the stepfather. She timidly searched the faces of the others in the dining area.

"Mom, men can talk about all kinds of things these days," Marty said.

"Listen to him. We're supposed to talk to each other like men, now," the stepfather scoffed.

"I'm just saying it is perfectly normal to bring up that subject in a humorous way," Marty continued.

"I'm glad we came to this restaurant. I hear the sausages are splendid," Mother said.

"I need to eat." The stepfather turned and gestured to the waiter.

"Don't get more drinks," Mother warned.

Stepfather glared at Mother for what seemed like many minutes.

"They made us wait an awfully long time. It's no wonder we've had more than our share of drinks," Marty said.

Stepfather ignored him and yelled at Mother, "Get outside now!"

The pair departed the restaurant leaving Marty to watch through the front window as they engaged in a silent, raging fight. Mother seemed to be giving the most violence. The stepfather stormed away but she chased after him. Marty turned and regarded the intricately folded napkin on his plate. He paid for the drinks and left without eating. He looked up the street as he emerged from the restaurant foyer. He spied the taco stand.

"I guess it's going to be home cooking for me today," Marty said.

Lynn Henderson stood before the register in a clothing store paying for a new pair of dark pants. She rolled up her bloodstained white pants and put them into a bag.

"I'm sorry you had to change in the toilet but we don't want a mess in the fitting area," the cashier said.

"You're out of paper in there," Lynn said.

Marty burst into the store setting the bells on the door clanging. "There's these Mexican guys after me," he said. He noticed Lynn. Their gazes embraced for a moment.

Two Mexican men in blue suits followed him into the store. The lean Mexican gestured to his partner.

"Let's go, kid," the short, bald Mexican said as he grabbed Marty. The three men left the store.

Marty soon found himself handcuffed to a beaten wood table inside a police interrogation room. The lean Mexican cop, Jesus, set a can of soda down and backed away to stare at Marty from the corner of the room.

The fat cop, Freddy, spoke, "We can sit here all night until you talk. Who changed the taco recipe?"

"Leave him, he's small time. They wouldn't tell him anything."

Marty whispered, "I remember I was in the lab and I heard a low, rumbling noise—"

Marty could see himself perched on the toilet holding his belly as it rumbled and lowed. His face was cold with sweat. He groaned and lifted his head. He cursed himself as he recalled his trip to the taco stand. He had ordered El Gigante.

"Hot and tangy fixings; you can design your own taco," he had remarked while poking a plastic spoon into the condiment tray. The onions and peppers had looked rotten and congealed with age. In the sunlight magnified by the Plexiglas sneeze guard clouds of flies hovered and darted through nauseating waves of gas. Marty had ignored his senses, images of the tantalizingly crunchy taco had overwhelmed him. He had spooned a liberal sampling of the condiments across his taco.

In the interrogation room, Marty could see himself balanced in the bathroom stall as the taste returned to him. He groaned. Whispering intensely, he tried to dash the memory with lies, "I heard a low, rumbling noise and I went out into the courtyard of the corporate park. I saw the seven board members mounting some sort of small airship.

I'd been working all night on the new bacon and fish taco. I was worn out. I know what I saw, though; something was very wrong about the whole setup. Who was I really working for? Why would they force me to put that chromium dust into the spice mix? They said it was a safe chemical preservative. I was too frightened to argue. What have I done?" Marty slumped forward. The cops were transfixed.

"Let it all out." Freddy patted his shoulder sympathetically.

"We want to help. Tell us everything you know," Jesus added.

Later, Marty stood in his underwear before a high-rise view of the city lights twinkling. He pressed his hand against his apartment window and lifted the telephone to speak, "I told them something I never dreamed could be true. It seemed as though they were waiting to hear it. There was a girl I saw just before they grabbed me. She was lovely. I almost torqued my nuts off just thinking about her hips. Please don't call me at home again." Marty walked back to his bed and sighed, "She's out there somewhere."

The seven board members were soaking naked in a warm fountain at the base of a terraced hill of cascading pools and gardens which sloped down from the patio of The Hacienda. The boss clipped his cell phone shut and looked up to the starry sky. "He's a good kid, that Marty. He took it like a man," the boss said.

Freddy, the fat cop, was at home with his wife. He was naked, sitting in the kitchen of their cheap barrio apartment. His wife, who could have been his twin save for the intrusion of her voluptuous figure and stunningly thick black locks, was methodically shaving the dense hair on Freddy's back. "There's no more nutmeg, so use mace instead. It's good for your tummy," she said.

Freddy heard her drop the razor and wail in horror. "What the fuck, baby?" Freddy asked.

"You ate at that taco stand again. I told you to stay away from that crappy gringo swill."

Freddy stood up to examine his back in the mirror. Beneath the shaved patch of hair he saw a small mouth puckering its lips at him, revealing sharp teeth.

Marty was restless in his bed that night. He was plagued by a staccato, dreaming sleep. He dreamed he was on the talk show again but this time he was sitting in the first chair, next to the host's desk.

"My next guest is a wonderful, talented new singer currently appearing at Broadway Square. Please welcome Miss Lynn Henderson," the host said.

Lynn emerged from between the stage curtains, resplendent in a red gown. Music arose as she took her mark. She lifted a microphone and began to sing:

> *I'm prettier than heaven is empty.*
> *I'm prettier than heaven is tall.*
> *But when I wear that glittering crown,*
> *I don't feel pretty at all.*
> *From the face of the earth,*
> *I could dance up to heaven.*
> *If I only could get the steps right.*
> *There's a song I could learn,*
> *It comes from somewhere,*
> *It contains every sound and the magic I need,*
> *It brings down the veil and the light.*

On the gravel and pitch roof of Taco World's headquarters the lean cop, Jesus, confronted the seven board members. They pressed towards him, Jesus was backed up to the edge of the roof. The boss was holding a ray gun.

"I'd love to stay and chat, amigos, my friends. Unfortunately, I don't have a visa so I fear I must deport myself from this rooftop," Jesus said. He kicked the ray gun from the boss's hand. He leapt at the outstretched branch of a nearby tree but his grasp failed. Jesus crashed awkwardly to the lawn below. The boss looked down at Jesus and turned to the other men, puzzled.

Jesus was dead on the lawn of the courtyard. The sun rose and birds of prey surrounded his body. The seasons changed. Jesus remained motionless under a thick snowfall. When spring returned strolling lovers passed his body. Happy children poked at him with sticks. Jesus decayed inexorably. Heavy summer rains washed his bones. A skeleton glowed beneath a full autumn moon.

Marty was eating donuts in the break room at the Taco World headquarters. Another junior chemist, Mel Willis, grabbed the last maple glazed donut. Marty stared at Mel's obesity bulging forth from an ill-fitting lab coat.

"When the wicked beareth rule, the people moveth," Mel said as he chewed the donut, pausing only to wipe icing from his beard. "I could take this whole place down with one phone call. I've been here nine years and I've seen many things far worse than mere safety code violations. An insurance conglomerate really owns this company. They have contracts with FEMA."

"Is that a conflict of interest?" Marty asked.

"You idiot, the head of FEMA is a member of The Carlton Group. They developed the red anthrax strain. Add it up."

The door to the break room opened and Lynn Henderson looked in at them both. "I'm sorry," she said. "I thought this was the legal department."

Marty stood up. He remembered Lynn's face.

"You look familiar. Do I know you?" Lynn asked.

"Not yet. Let me show you how to get to Legal. It's hard to find one's way around this place. You're in the wrong building," Marty said. He escorted Lynn outside. They walked and chatted together amiably, comfortably.

They climbed a set of wide stone steps which lead to the main office courtyard. The seven board members bounded past them down the steps. The men were dressed in tennis whites and casual shoes.

"Who are those gay fellows?" Lynn asked.

"Believe it or not, they run this company," Marty informed her.

"What a fun place to work!" Lynn said.

"I think you will like it here," Marty said as he touched Lynn's hand.

16

SHOULD THIS MAN
DESERVE AN AUTOBIOGRAPHY?

When he pulled into the gas station he was too tired from driving to fully assess the locale. He walked in unprepared. The glass walls of the little store were rendered opaque by the lights shining from the pump island canopy.

Once inside, he understood the scene: the owner, the mother, forcing her daughter to work on a Friday night. The girl watched him.

"Are you coming back from the Garth Brooks concert?" She asked.

"I'm driving through. I saw the stadium lights, though." He handed over money for gasoline.

"I couldn't go to the concert." The girl turned east and jabbed her head towards her mother who was stocking a soda cooler. "She says I'm too young."

"They might stop in here and get gasoline. It could be your lucky day."

He walked to the restrooms in the back. On the floor near the urinals he saw a case of diet soda. A few cans were gone. Back at the front of the store he took it upon himself to mention it to the owner. Maybe some kids on their way to the concert had been maximizing their night out with a little shoplifting.

He always tried to make the most of an opportunity to connect with strangers in a decent way. It was simple to stand together and talk across the barrier of the unknown while watching football scores and weather on television in the drivers' lounge or while standing on the street as an ambulance carted someone away. In crowds, we can touch each other. Out here in this stretch of Ohio highway farmland, the part of Ohio he always failed to incorporate into his perpetual map of the state (his current edition was dominated by the water cities like

Cleveland and Toledo), out here in the center of a placid transaction
the effort of reporting this crime could have a spreading effect, like the
detonation of a shotgun shell underwater.

"There's a case of soda in the washroom. Looks like someone was
trying to steal it, maybe some kids," he said.

The mother stared at him and said, "We use that case of soda to
hold the door open when we clean the toilets."

Back out on the road he tried to call Michigan but his cell phone
battery was dead. He'd wanted to talk with Marie, to apologize for the
way he'd acted the last time he saw her. She had taken him to the art
museum and he had been repulsed.

It had been a traveling exhibit, she'd paid for tickets, groups were let
in every twenty minutes. In front of each painting there were clusters of
people holding audio devices up to their heads. The collection was the
property of some rich guy who began buying things after a personal
tragedy left a void in his life. He had filled that void with a heavy dose
of 19th century French painting, a few later pieces; the collection was
a series of postcards from a rich young man's transatlantic crossing and
grand tour.

He'd learned all about it from some wall text that he'd had his
face pressed against while trying to sneak around the mob transfixed
before the jaunty Renoir which dominated the center of the show like
a neon bowl of horse piss. More wall text had explained that "just as
the items in your shopping cart at the grocery store tell a story about
who you are, so the collector represents the shadows of his inner life by
his selection and pursuits."

He had walked to the end of the exhibit and tracked through it
backwards hoping to spend a moment or two alone with the paintings
before another twenty minutes passed. He'd examined a pair of
contrasting still lifes meant to depict the transition from the dark
oaken precision of Chardin's interior design schemes to the brighter
but inescapably rigorous oppression of bath towel, kitchen tile and
light marble countertop themes scraped directly from Cezanne's
palette. Near the entrance he'd made eye contact with a small but
vibrant El Greco until a click of the latch on a velvet rope had signaled
the approach of the next bunch of visitors.

Hot and uncomfortable, feeling as though he was holding the line up at a bank, he'd dodged his way forward and finally found Marie. She was angry because she had expected to stroll through the exhibit with him. She was further offended when he had said, "it was just a dehumanizing cattle drive past some rich prick's investment portfolio." He had compared the exhibit to "the hideous Christmastime house tour that the stupid slobs in this city put on every year."

I hadn't known at the time that Marie had planned to take me down along the park the next day and lead me through that very same holiday tour.

I never saw those splendid houses and now I believed the cell phone dysfunction was a pivotal sign. I resolved to leave things with Marie where they were. I would take responsibility for what I had said. I would live it through.

I started this off by telling a story about "HE"—I realize that. I tried to put a little space between my agenda and the reader into which I could cast a few cold comments as I conspired with you to point out the unreasonably selfish and closed attitude of this "HE" character so that our mutual bemusement would effectively suggest poignant conclusions about confidence in the presence of adversity.

I don't know why I tried to do it that way. It seemed unnatural to speak directly about such jarringly patent inequities when the course of this story leads to a simple conflict. It is a conflict between myself and the accomplishments that have taken root around me, which seek to dominate me and compel me to compete and render stronger accomplishments with my own life.

I'm confused by the choice between building something that is profound or building up and maintaining the image of something profound. It does seem that the path of generating the aura of accomplishment has a flaw that is the deathly need for recognition of authorship; an autobiography of indirect genius that leaves no monument to posterity unless it bears the name or likeness of the man.

It seems a path I cannot follow. I feel put down, especially when I'm sitting naked on the edge of my bed cleaning my toes with a pair of dirty underwear I have just used to wipe away any remnants from my butt. I might be unworthy to present as a figure to whom one day would be ascribed, for example, the commission of an early design by a future titan of urban architecture.

Much of this confusion entered my life after reading *The Autobiography of Benvenuto Cellini*. I bought it at a used bookstore. The cashier, a part-time libertine who did layout work for specialty porn magazines, found the volume and handed it over with a sneer, "Here it is: Benvenuto 'Suh-Lee-Nee.'" I thanked him.

A year later, I heard the name in conversation and suffered a delayed slash of mortification. More importantly, I read the book and I learned about "Chuh-Lee-Nee" and became obsessed by the human need (Ben Franklin wrote of this) to "do something worth the writing." Alive in one part of your brain you could move through your days on a crooked line in pursuit of some temporally substantial goal while another part of your brain recorded unflinchingly the pathetic influence of the pursuit of identity.

I could not judge the quality of worth. Did these stories last so long in our history because they contained a spiraled calculus, a helix which could unleash the confidence and strength that was potential in any human willing to challenge the daunting obstacle of absorbing an entire human life from the page and thereby ritually consuming and carrying forward that soul? It was not a universal interest, this possibility; a certain cast of ego forced a person to live that way. And if there was dishonesty lurking in the belly of a man who consumed the lives of old it made a sickness, a chronic infection which made death a finality without echo.

I arrived at my home in Pennsylvania and I was thinking about apologizing to Marie. I turned on my PC hoping to research the life of the art collector I had disparaged with such grotesque and illegitimate haste. I considered that my bad mood at the exhibit had perhaps stemmed from the mistake of not putting my coat and sweater into one of the museum's lockers before I got in line. If I could find some facts about the art collector I could express to Marie a little more respectful and sympathetic appreciation for the man who chose to bring great European paintings home for Americans to see. He could have created a lot of mischief with all that money and freedom but maybe instead he had founded rural art schools or carted his collection around by train to display for the residents of mining towns in Idaho.

I never found anything about him, I didn't really have a chance to look. When I called Marie later I spoke to her with those nobly forgiving images in mind, and I did manage to smooth things out. She agreed to fly out and visit me. I would plan some day trips for us; there had to be some sort of mansion tour in this area, there had to be at least one house with a fifty-foot-high wooden door.

I never did my research on the art collector because while I was trying to open my internet browser I opened a folder of old email by mistake. I could not remember the person who had written them. The address did not suggest a nickname I was familiar with and there were no headers or signatures attached so I opened them one by one and started to read:

> "I had to cut back on the weed because the service light in my truck is on. I talked to Jules yesterday and he said he talked to your ex-wife. I pried a little for you and it seems she invited him out to Portland. Trust me, he couldn't tell I was checking up on her. Was your divorce brutal or are you still friends with her? Give me a call, I'd like to talk.
>
> Buzzard is moving to Bayton County, he's the last friend I had on the construction crew I work for. All I have left are beers and weed. I haven't been practicing my karate because it is so fucking hot here, 103 degrees today. I cut back on work since I got this house-sitting job so I can stay stoned all the time. I've been shitting better. Your ex-wife is amazingly fucked up. Did you have to sue her? I found out I was born with a deformity. I have an extra bone in my sinus and that's why my forehead sticks out sometimes. No phone calls from you yet, fuck you, that's fine. I'm sure you're still real busy dealing with your new living arrangements. If I come up there to visit Jules can take a bus down from Albany. I told him he can't stay at your place and he's cool with that.
>
> I've been taking painkillers but they don't give me a buzz, they just get rid of the sinus pain. Right now, I can only work two days out of every week. It's still hot, 105 degrees yesterday. I'm so broke I

might be able to qualify for free healthcare. If not I'm going to have to do something drastic, maybe sell one of my motorcycles. I was going to mail you some videos but all I have is your old address and I don't want your ex-wife to end up with them. Jules came back into town and we went out drinking with his sister. He took her home afterward and later I found out she fell down in the shower and cracked her skull—dead. She has a little kid and I'm really worried he either saw it happen or discovered the body. Before that night I hadn't had a drink in three weeks and now I'm physically sick, guilty and angry. This is what I've been dealing with, I'm going to stop drinking again. Is your divorce final yet? It would suck if she wins again and gets everything after all the shit that bitch pulled on you. You're really the winner because you will grow as a human being.

I'm back to working six days every week, amen. I need to buy a cell phone and put some money into fixing my truck. This city is really expensive compared to what I make. Plus, what is the point of living here when I hardly ever go out? I'm thinking of selling a couple motorcycles so I'll be ready to move out of here when the time is right. They sold my grandmother's house. I got a little wistful, I think I masturbated in every room of that house at one time or another. Carol is giving me a lot of shit, lately. Now that she's stopped drinking she's a bigger bitch than ever, lectures me all the time. She still likes a little white wine with dinner. I have been distancing myself from her. I feel guilty about it but she makes me want to drink. I tried calling your old phone number and I talked to your ex-wife, briefly. She said you hadn't been there for a while and that she had a call on the other line. My feelings about Carol are only worry and pity. My cock is so backed up, I've been playing a lot of videogames to keep my mind off it.

I had two beers last night and wrote a threatening email to Jules, that asshole can't break his promises fast enough. The beer made me shit blood. I might have to switch to something thick and sweet like a cherry liqueur. How is your ex-wife doing? I'm really worried about her. Send her my love if you talk to her. Carol called me for the first time in three weeks. She needed me to drive her to the gynecologist, she only has a bicycle. I'll always be there to help her out but I sometimes feel like I should get laid in return. I wish I could be decent. She's great but we're not good together. I had some work done on my teeth so I got codeine. With the pills I can cut down to three beers a week. I was over at my dad's house and I managed not to pass out in his lounge chair. Things are looking up.

I went by Carol's house to drop off some beer and frozen pizza. The guy at the grocery store only charged me two dollars for everything. He said: 'the people have to stick together.' I slept over at Carol's, we downed all the pizza and beer and then had sex. After she fell asleep I started farting all night. Her mattress must still be scorched from both the gas and my grinding groin. I hadn't felt so rested in a long time but all peace was shattered when my butt started leaking what looked like transmission fluid. I had food poisoning, probably from the 'freedom' pizza.

I've been staying at my dad's house until I get better. I got some more pills from the doctor. I have to sneak out into the backyard to smoke weed. I haven't been out to see Carol in two weeks. She's looking pretty old. What's going on with the divorce? Are you going to get the house? Give me a call, I'm feeling pretty low. I have to make some big changes in my life. At the doctor's office I was getting pretty tight with the brunette nurse. I keep fantasizing about getting a hand job from her while I'm lying in a hospital bed attached to life-support. I think I must have smelled needy to her so nothing really happened between us. I was at the doctor's office because of this recurring flatulence I have due to the food poisoning. I picked up some more painkillers as well as cortisone for my sinus condition so I can get back to work. I'm going to apply for healthcare assistance from the county. I might be able to get a 'workman's compensation' benefit. I'll have to smack my knee with a brick at the jobsite to give some visible wounds; combined with everything else that should make the grade.

I talked to Janine (your ex-wife's friend) and we caught up on everything. Listening to my own stories I started thinking I should be writing them down on index cards, one or two every day. I forget things. Janine asked a lot of questions about you, sounded like your ex-wife put her up to it. I didn't give up any information. If you hear any rumors about yourself they didn't come from me."

I finished reading the last note and I went to bed while the sun was coming up. I was vexed, trying to piece this human together as I drifted off to sleep. I was restless because I was the only person who owned this collection. If I were to destroy it maybe I'd be doing the author a favor but it felt like an awesome responsibility. They couldn't have wanted all that information sitting there; it was private and personal but that's what made it honest, authentic. If I printed it out I could keep it alive; maybe he deserved that.

17

KNUCKLEBALLER

Yankee Stadium: St. Louis v. New York, Game 6

The knuckleball glided to home plate. It moved unpredictably along currents of air but stayed up in the zone. The batter narrowed his vision. The bat uncoiled, shocking the hesitant five-ounce orb with the rude force of heroic assurance. The ball accelerated back to the mound. It smashed off the pitcher's cheekbone and ricocheted into right field. As the pitcher fell to the ground he heard the crowd noise explode. It was all over.

I was sitting in a bar in Memphis when a man walked near my table and stopped. I didn't look up past his belt. I stared at my drink. A minute passed and he moved on. St. Louis used to have a huge following down here. They covered most of the south on the radio. A lot of people still follow them. I hoped I hadn't been recognized. I'd avoided wearing my cap all through this trip. I look very different without my cap. Memphis is on highway forty in Tennessee. I had stopped here for a drink, with an eye towards getting into a hotel. My face still hurt.

Right after we lost, I stayed in the hospital for a while, maybe even a little longer than I should have. I was in a very bad mood because I was stuck in New York all through the victory celebrations. The hour I was released from the hospital I rented a car and rode out to Atlantic City. I made the papers in New York again.

I had been in Atlantic City for a week, only about twenty-thousand down at blackjack. In the lounge, I struck up a conversation with a card player from Texas. One thing led to another and pretty soon we were in my suite. He did a couple lines just to stay up. I didn't partake.

He was showing me how he could count into a shoe. I had a few decks of souvenir cards and Texas was showing off, hitting hand after hand.

We hatched a plan as the sun came up. I would bankroll him. I thought I had the guy figured. He was just an animal save for this one skill. I wanted vengeance for my loss. That brought the whole program crashing down. I pushed him into playing larger stakes. He protested but I had the money. I watched him from a chair in the slots. We got way ahead. The pit boss came up and tapped him on the shoulder. I got a sick feeling when I realized they seemed to know this guy. They pulled him away from the table. A posse of dark suits took my money and led Texas into the back. I followed them to where the official part of the casino started but they would not let me pass.

I retreated into the lounge, silently mouthing the word "fuck" and slamming down the drink "gin." I decided to go back to the offices and talk to the head of security, I thought maybe he would recognize me. I felt certain that I could come up with an explanation that would get back my fifty-thousand dollars. Looking back, I'm not quite clear on the logic, I hadn't slept for nearly three days. I crossed briskly through the casino floor and back to the guard station. An argument ensued. The guard did not agree with my interpretation of casino rules. I kicked the guard and broke into a dead run through the grand lobby. I was hoping I could jump in a car and get out of there. A parking attendant was just pulling up outside when I hit the street. I pushed him down and yelled: 'It's okay, I'm a cop.' As the security force burst out of the casino, I threw the car into reverse, gunned it and jumped the back end into a massive, lighted fountain.

I was locked up for a couple of days. I finally gave a much more reasonable explanation of my actions, omitting the part about my association with the card-counter. I think Texas tried to nark me out but my lawyers, in their last official act on my behalf, shut that down. I phoned my agent and discovered that I had been released by St. Louis. He went on to add that he would no longer represent me.

As winter dragged on, I worked my way through the southern casinos. I came to believe I needed a year off. I felt like I was into something very healing. Age wouldn't ruin me, my pitching was all nerve. I pressed on with my journey. So far, I had made it to Tennessee.

Spring training started on the day I pulled into the driveway of my house. Just before the playoffs, I had purchased the house through my investment adviser, Pete Rugolo. I had wanted to live in my spring training city. So here I was and I just sat there. To cheer me up, Pete started to come by and sit with me. He would tell me about the players he had as clients. A little at a time, I started giving him insights into an athlete's needs. Pete seemed to respect my judgment. The knuckleball pitcher has to develop a strong faith and strange senses. I started to think that I could use my knuckleball mind to work with Pete and The Rugolo Corporation.

Rugolo handled a little bit of everything: media, investment and construction. The company had grown out of a publishing firm Pete's dad had run that put out girlie and biker mags, hot rod mags and humor stuff like *CARtoons*. They had moved out here in the fifties and seemed to have invested in every golden opportunity since. Consequently, Pete was at the root of this town.

Pete started sending me out to meet people. I would tell a few stories, have some drinks. I took a read on each man like I was pitching to him. I delivered my impressions to Pete. It's hard for the average person to understand how consuming baseball is to a pro; especially to a pro like me: not a natural, getting by on balls and brains. It had all come undone and I was forced to work in the square world. I vowed to approach it with the same tenacity that had taken me so high in baseball. I found strength returning.

Pete called me and set up a private meeting. I had been working with him for a few months. Judging by the praise I was getting from Pete, I figured that this was a meeting of intimacy. He was drawing me closer.

Pete cleared his throat. "You've seen a lot of what goes on around here and that's pretty rare. You know I don't let a lot of people in. You were useful to me because as a ball player you provide a certain glamour to my business and that attracts people. There is more, you can read people. In my business there are advantages to be had and this kind of information is valuable to me. I wanted to sit you down and maybe deepen our relationship."

"You've helped me get my confidence back. I'm glad I have something to offer," I said.

"The truth is that you're helping yourself financially. You have a lot of your money in my businesses. I'm not sure you know how much. The paychecks have dropped off for you and I think it's time to get a little more involved with your investments. You have a certain skill, a way of sneaking up on people before they can get their defenses up. I have seen it. You could be helping me by using this skill in a more active role."

"I've been putting my energy into this, Pete. I'm glad you noticed."

"I have noticed, believe me. I don't come to this decision lightly. I want you to work for me full-time as a personal consultant." Pete moved around to my side of the desk. "I would like to give you more responsibility."

"I'm very interested in that," I said.

"You know my wife, Janine? She is instrumental in making my business work. She manages the details in my real estate investments. Did you know that? She plays a big part. She handles the construction. I'm getting busy with other things. I have to travel a lot. These trends look to continue. I have fallen out of touch with what she handles. I need you to watch her for me. Keep me informed. I think you would be very good at that."

"I could do it," I said.

"She tells me things: numbers, dates, what have you. What I want is a feeling for how she carries things out. She's sharp. She's unpredictable. Her behavior is a reflection on the business as a whole. Janine knows how to get things done. I want to know more about how she does them."

Having been down here for a while I knew what he meant. Growth in this area depended on a very tightly constricted pact between developers and government. The tender balance struck by these forces was critical to any goal. I nodded my head as Pete continued.

"The time has come. I'm not around much. I need to know how things are being handled. We can't push too hard. Janine might need a little restraint. I need to know when to apply it. I need someone watching her very closely. She's hotheaded. She's pushy. She lacks a certain amount of respect. My business requires careful strategy. I've tried to talk with her but it's not my place as a husband. Then there's you. With what you've shown me, I believe you can handle this situation. We need to know what she does; not to interfere, just to know."

Pete looked frustrated. Sensing that we had covered everything, I stood up. "Don't say another word. I accept the job. You will have access now. Don't worry."

We shook hands and we would stand on that handshake. I meant what I had said to Pete. I owed him a lot. Pete was about twenty-five years older than Janine. They were like a father and a daughter in many ways. Like a father, Pete had protective instincts. It was perfectly reasonable to want to know how Janine was carrying herself. There was only the question of how I would come through for him that vexed me. In baseball, there are only winning and losing. In this new game complexities would emerge. I knew I couldn't control the ball, I could only control my relationship to it. It was all in the grip.

The next day, I went by Pete's office and he was glaring at the telephone. It was ringing, Pete let it ring on.

"Do you know who it is?" I asked.

"Janine." Pete shook his head.

"I'm not going to answer the phone," I said.

"Whatever you want," Pete said. The answering machine picked up the call. "The sound of her voice makes me queasy. Turn the speaker down on that thing."

"I'm listening to the message."

"Why didn't you answer it?" Pete asked.

"It's Marino Tijeras," I said, holding my hand up to Pete.

"Sounds like a woman."

"He's looking for Janine," I explained.

"Her voice gets to me. It makes me feel like she's about to ask a favor."

"I should call him?" I asked Pete.

"I don't know anything about it," he said.

"Marino mentioned Springwood. What is that?"

"That is exactly why I need you. I've been out of town so much I have lost track. I remember the property but I can't tell you where we are with it." Pete started searching his desk.

"Why is Marino asking about it? I thought he was just a working stiff."

"When you used to know him, he was. He worked for me off and on, did some time. His brother is in the church, though, and Janine took up a request from that realm. She showed some mercy and made a project out of the boy."

"He was a good kid," I recalled.

"But this is what concerns me, this kind of thing. She helps him out; does she have to promote the guy to contracting? I'm not running a charity. Janine gets involved with everyone's problems. I haven't seen her in a few weeks. She's always rushing around to a job site or cleaning up someone else's mess."

"I'll run by and talk to Marino. I'll start there and follow up. Anything else is just worry, at this point." I jotted down Tijeras' number. I still remembered where he lived. This was what I had needed, something specific. I had planned on having to interview Pete for a while to get a feel for the situation, maybe even go through some files. I didn't want to just start following Janine around, first thing.

I went to Marino Tijeras' apartment but he swore he hadn't seen Janine all day. "I left a message with Pete to check if she was on her way over here," he said.

"She never got it," I said.

"If you see her, tell her she better pay me."

"I don't care," I said.

"You can believe I need that money, right?"

"I can believe you need the money."

"Janine called me earlier. She was going to stop at the train station. She had to ride up to Halifax and meet somebody about landscaping. She doesn't want Pete to know. After that she was coming over here. She never came," Marino said.

"Pete knows all about it," I lied.

"If he expects me to do the Springwood job, I have to get paid what she owes."

"Is this money she owes from something else?"

"Back pay. I did that job good and I've got people, man. Tell Pete, ask him if he'd pay my bill. His name's on the permit."

"I'll mention it." I walked around Marino's apartment while we talked. He stayed seated in front of the TV, watching the news with the sound off.

"I don't want Pete pissed at me. That fucking Janine is crazy sometimes but she moves the cash around. Pete will just sit on it and give all the work to his pals. I want to be in business. I'm not going to be fucking off." Marino stopped talking when the TV displayed a sketch of a man wanted in connection to a spate of recent abortion clinic bombings here in the city. He laughed. "That drawing stinks. You can't tell if he's Mexican or white."

"How are things otherwise?" I asked.

"Can't complain." Marino was transfixed by the TV.

I decided to swing by my house on the way to the train station. I thought I'd check out Marino's story and then head out to Springwood. At the very least, I'd get a sense of the terrain I'd be inhabiting from now on. I drank a beer and ate a cold pork chop over the sink.

I drove over to the train station and circled through the parking decks. I parked across the street from the train station. I took notes on a Chinese restaurant menu that I had in the glove compartment: an older couple escorting three young girls; a quartet of teenagers dressed alike, determined looks on their faces; a red-haired guy; young woman, big hair, probably going to the hockey game. I noticed a church next to the station. It had one of those neon crosses with lettering: "We preach Christ crucified." I hadn't been down in this part of the city for a while, it had come up in the world. Nobody else came out of the station, no trace of Janine. I called Marino on my cell phone. I got no answer and hung up. I checked the time and wrote that down. I drove around the parking decks again and headed home.

When I got back I turned the security system on. I thumbed through the evening newspaper. There was a big article on the abortion clinic bombings. I went into the front room and sank into my leather couch. I seated myself facing the TV but as I hadn't gotten around to hooking up the cable, it was a pointless choice. I watched my silhouette in the black mirror of the screen.

I dreamt some strange, nasty dreams sleeping cramped up in that chair. My house was too hot. The shock of the air outside made me recognize the fetid steam from which I had emerged. I tried to focus on the chore of driving through traffic to Springwood. I tried not to think about what Janine was getting into. Pete wanted me to watch her, not to fix her.

When Pete had a problem, getting other people involved in it made it more visceral for him. Sitting there and having it grind him down was not his way to take it. He wanted action, no matter how worthless.

While I was pitching, the other guys in the bullpen tried to spread their problems around. When the ball wasn't biting, it helped to get your mind off it. I usually didn't have much to talk about. I couldn't blame anything if I was on a losing streak. I could barely even blame myself. I was out there along with everyone else in the park just watching my pitches unfold. Sometimes the batter seemed to know more about them than I did. As long as I kept my motion consistent I was doing my best. I will always be able to play the mental game but now my left eye isn't right. And I'm getting fat.

I arrived at Springwood and Pete was there, smoking a cigar. "Janine's in some kind of hot water. She left another message last night, I think," Pete said.

"You wouldn't answer the phone?"

"That's your job now."

"I didn't make it by here yesterday. Any news?" I asked.

"Did you just sit home all night?"

"I've been running around." I said.

"I hear that." Pete thrust his cigar in my direction.

"Janine seems to be getting behind on some of her invoices," I said.

"We need to start pouring concrete here soon and I have to go to Lexington tonight." Pete put the cigar back into his mouth. The conversation was over.

I crossed through the site into the model home. I watched Pete through the window while I called out from the sales office to Marino Tijeras' apartment. Looking around as the phone rang I saw that the model home was showing a lot of wear. It could have been the workers, the security guards, or maybe Janine camping out here from time to time. I'd have to keep an eye on it.

Janine answered the phone at Marino's place. "I heard you were looking for me, knuckleballer," she said.

"Pete gave me a promotion. I'm helping him with Springwood, since he's been so busy."

"I'm glad things are working out for you. You should come down here and I'll show you what I have on it."

"Is Marino around?"

"He went up to Star City."

"Did you work everything out with him?"

"You're going to learn a lot about the construction business," she said. "Nothing is ever on time and no one gets what they want."

"If I can bring Pete some figures it would make me look good, unless you were going to be seeing him soon. It would probably make more sense coming from you."

"We're both so slammed, right now. Once we get this job started things will calm down. You might as well do your thing."

"I appreciate that," I said.

"We're getting Tijeras' crew to do the job but he isn't Pete's favorite guy. We'll save a lot of money this way but that won't convince Pete. He wants you to be in the middle just in case he needs to push the board to use his guys. There are always considerations that must be paid but Pete doesn't realize things are changing around here. Did you know that Marino has a relative on the City Council? I need to bring this thing in for a landing without interference. Once Pete sees the returns he'll be happy but right now I have to keep my distance," Janine said.

"I'll come meet you and take a crash course," I said.

"You'll get that all right. I have to get off the phone with you and make some other calls." As she hung up I felt a flush of security. I was the stopper coming in from the bullpen. I could be the ace. I needed to keep Pete comfortable about what Janine was doing, without giving anything away. With Janine I had merely to be straight forward and she'd give me access. I could help the whole thing resolve. Pete was long gone by the time I got back to my car. I felt the sunshine for the first time today. I could trust my instincts again. Janine was crafty, Pete was right but he knew her better than he wanted to admit. The loyalty they shared had to be strong to survive the kind of business they did. I could see that, now. Theirs' was not a career for choirboys. I knew Janine was mouthy, she could put you to sleep with her non-stop lines of bullshit. It helped in negotiations. I'd never seen her get pulled up short. She just shifted gears and took off in the open lane.

Last winter, I had stayed at Pete's house for a week. One day we were having a cookout and I went upstairs to use the washroom. I opened the wrong door. Janine was there smoking a cigarette, sitting on the edge of the bed. She was wearing nothing but a bra and panties. She looked pretty good. She had a pack of Newports stuck in her bra strap. It almost ruined the effect. She didn't look at me and I turned to leave. "There's no furniture in here. I need to keep track of these cigs. It's my last pack." Janine said as she unhooked her bra. "Take these out with you. Don't lose them." She threw the cigarettes across the room and they hit me in the chest. I got it together, picked up the cigarettes and left. She could handle herself fine. Pete just needed to be patient and remember that.

The traffic on the freeway was a drag. I missed Janine but she had left me an envelope on Marino's door. Inside were copies of spread-sheets, work orders and handwritten notes. I could settle down with it tonight and really bust my cherry in the construction trade. With Pete out of town this was a perfect time to find the strike zone.

I took the surface roads back home and I went past the train station again. In the gravel lot beside the "Christ Crucified" church I saw Marino's car. Something was wrong with that, he should have been in Star City.

I pulled myself over a wall of corrugated metal at the back of the lot. There was a pipe rail along the side of the church and I stood on it to look into the closest window. Marino was inside with a priest and two other guys. They were tinkering with what looked like a batch of shattered radios. Before I could register anything else, someone grabbed my legs and pulled me off the rail. I went down face first into the sidewalk. A warm, red veil fell across my eyes as something hard smacked the back of my head.

I thought it was midnight. I couldn't see a goddam thing. I tried to move my hands up to my eyes but there was a black weight upon me. I started to think that I had landed on some jagged metal, crushed my eyes and gone blind. I kicked my knees up and I could see light. I lifted myself slowly. I found that I had been stashed under a thick tarp. I had been flattened out in the back of a truck parked in the church lot. The back door to the church was open. The sun was still out but heading down.

A wave of pain and sickness made my skin go cold. Sweat had soaked my clothes and hair. I had been under the tarp all afternoon. The chill passed and I fell back onto the hot metal of the truck bed. The tarp fell back over me. I didn't have the strength to push it away. I lay there taking in short hot breaths, wishing I would blackout again. I hovered there with a ringing in my ears. I moaned as best I could with my mouth smothered against the heavy cloth.

I woke again. It wasn't as hot now. What brought me out was a solid drumming at my temples, a dull second round of pain. I tried to catalog my injuries. My face was tender but my teeth felt intact. I tried to fold my left leg up and there I found the source of the throbbing in my brain. My broken ankle was pushed flat by the weight of the tarp. By moving my leg slowly, this way and that, I was able to trim the pain into a nice even drone. I pushed the tarp away from my face. The sun was down. I took a good gasp of air. I was almost strong enough to move out of there.

I heard gravel crunch. Marino Tijeras was leaning over me. His crucifix swept down and brushed across my face.

"You're out of shape," he said.

"What the hell is going on?" I mumbled.

"Some of the neighborhood kids fucked you up. They took your money. We found you collapsed out there like a sack of garbage." Marino pointed towards the street.

"Are you working here?"

"We do church jobs for half price. Giving something back to the community." He put his hand on my shoulder as I tried to sit up.

"Let me up. I need to get to the hospital." I reached for my ankle.

"It isn't broken, you pussy, probably just twisted it. I tried to call Pete for you but there was no answer."

"You should have called an ambulance," I explained.

"We were too busy, just then, so we set you out here and we got started doing something."

"You cocksuckers. I was back here all day with the sun cooking my ass."

"We covered you up so the sun wouldn't burn you too bad. It was hot today."

"Good thinking."

"I had a nice silk shirt on but you got blood on it. I always need to wear a t-shirt under there anyway so I don't get chafed from the crucifix. I got this in Guadalupe." He held up the cross so I could inspect it.

"It's beautiful. Help me out of here."

Marino kissed the cross and let it drop. He helped me slide down to the edge of the truck bed. I put a little weight on my foot and was surprised to find it wasn't that bad. "I fell off that railing over there," I said, pointing back to the church. "I thought maybe Janine was in there."

"The railing, that explains it. Those kids must have took you for a meth-head thief. They love beating the shit out of those fucks. I respect that. They keep the scum out of the neighborhood. Why would Janine be here?"

"The Springwood job, I thought your guys would have been all over that."

"Did she mention that she was going to come by?"

"I think so."

"She didn't come here. I think she's looking to regret messing with me."

"She likes your work. She wants you to do more for her."

"Go home and sleep. You're probably a little confused." Marino walked back towards the church.

I heard the church door slam behind the fence. I stood there like an idiot for a few minutes and then started to walk up the street towards my car.

I found my wallet, the cash had been stolen but nothing else. They had gone through my car. The papers Janine had left me were gone and so was my cell phone. A cab pulled away from the train station and I saw a crowd waiting there. I recognized one of the men I had seen last night. It was an older guy with obviously dyed red hair. He noticed I was watching him just as another cab pulled in. He turned and headed down the alley between the church and the train station. I limped after him as fast as I could but he was gone and the alley was empty.

On the way home, I started remembering what I had seen before I got knocked out. Marino had been working on some electrical equipment. He was lying. He had even made a threat to Janine. Maybe he was using threats to get those jobs from her. Janine could have been in deep, hiding it from Pete. If Marino wasn't intimidating her with violence maybe he was using his city council connection. I needed to see those papers Janine left for me. And that redheaded guy knew who I was and he knew I saw him. I couldn't concentrate. When I got home I shut it down.

I woke up late in the afternoon the next day and washed some Vicodin down with a beer. They would provide little relief but it was nice to avoid feeling the pain for a few hours. I decided that those two vikes would be my last until I actually got some bones broken. I was feeling a little dry in the mind. When Sandy Koufax retired, and not too many people remember this, one of his major complaints was how much seconal he needed to make his starts. The pains I had were minimal so I would skip the meds from now on. I needed my wits about me. Maybe I would finally hook the cable up to my TV and watch a ball game. I'd been paying the cable company for six months. I got it all up and running. I checked out the news. I was staggered when I saw there had been another abortion clinic bombing, this time in Star City. It could have been the pills but it made sense: could Marino Tijeras be the bomber? He was Catholic, I noticed the electrical equipment, they were gone from the church all day, mister red hair ran away when he saw me. Janine must be involved in some way, Marino must have pulled her in. If Pete had suspected something this big I could understand why he was worried. As I hovered there, the phone rang.

"Listen, I saw you last night. I know who you work for," a voice said.

"Marino, is that you?" I asked.

"Never mind."

"Who is this?"

"You looked pretty bad last night."

"I'm going to hang up now," I said.

"I'll be watching you. Good luck, knuckleballer."

He hung up. I was contemplating the possibility of ripping the phone out of the wall when it rang again. I grabbed it quick, "Don't play games with me, fuck. You've crossed the line."

"Is this Pizza Supreme?"

"Wrong number."

No more telephones tonight. I looked around the room for something heavy to drop on it. Then I remembered I could just switch on my answering machine. It was one of those old cassette models so it would also work nicely as a sledgehammer. I was weighing the pros and cons of venting my general frustration on the phone when I realized that my answering machine was gone.

I got up painfully and searched the house. I couldn't recall precisely the sequence of events after I got home last night but I was pretty sure it didn't include throwing my answering machine out the window. Someone had stolen it. I examined the security system. I had forgotten to turn it on. I looked around the house but nothing else seemed to be missing. It had to be that red haired little prick from the train station. He was the joker in the deck. I went outside and turned the whole goddam system on, including the floodlights around the edge of my property and the electric fence. Mister Red Hair was more than welcome to try to get back inside. This time he'd get a nice surprise. I grabbed my shotgun and some shells. I slept lightly.

I woke up early and started some coffee. I needed a plan of attack. Pete would be returning and I wanted to be able to present him with the full story. He deserved as much from me. As the morning juice brewed I went upstairs to shower and change. Checking myself in the mirror I was pleased to see that my facial wounds looked dignified. Shaving was out of the question.

It was another hot day so I went with the cotton and silk in sharp purple and white. I hoped to offset my disfigurements with style. I would go to the city clerk and then to Rugolo Corporation itself and do some research. I needed to look professional and a little menacing.

I'd talk to Marino. Maybe he'd tried to get to Pete, told him something, lies. I couldn't do anything about Mister Red Hair, just try and lose him.

I guided my car south, heading toward Marino's apartment. In the time I had known Marino Tijeras I hadn't learned much about him. He was a longtime citizen affecting the manners of an illegal. He lived in that part of town. He worked and partied in that style. I parked one block from Marino's building. It was a blazing morning but I felt good parked here in the shade drinking Jarritos and chewing on a chile relleno. The heat soothed my wounds. I might be strong enough to run a few blocks at top speed today. I might chase someone or get chased. I hoped to catch Marino leaving, by following him around I might learn something. There had been one thing about Marino I had noticed, he was graceful. One time we all went to a rodeo. Out of nowhere he pulls up to Pete's with a bottle of wine. He talked us into the car and next thing you know we were driving a hundred miles to see rodeo under the lights. Then there was this thing with the church and Janine. I had a lot to learn about him, still.

I wiped my lips clean of chile grease. Seeing my face in the rearview mirror I realized there was one thing I had in common with Marino, we were both stubborn; feeling good about something you held as moral, worshipping commitment. Still staring into the mirror, I noticed some movement at the front door of Marino's building. Not the departure I had expected to see; instead, the arrival of two cops. One was in uniform, the other wore a suit.

I followed into the building. They were in his apartment. They must have put him together with the clinic bombings like I had. I walked back to the taqueria and dialed the pay phone.

"Talk to me," said the cop.

"Can I speak to Tijeras?"

"Who is this?"

"Ben Roberts, from the church. I was supposed to get a load of lumber from him today."

"Mr. Roberts, I'm afraid he won't be keeping that appointment. Right now, his apartment is a crime scene. We're searching for Mr. Tijeras ourselves. Did you speak with him recently?"

"I saw him yesterday. He is working with us, renovating the church."

"What is the name of the church?"

"Grace Christ Crucified," I said.

"I'd like to send someone over there. If you could give us a statement it would help."

"I'll be here at the church all day," I said. "I hope Mr. Tijeras turns up."

"So do we." Despite his implacable voice the cop seemed excited when I connected Marino to the church for him. My suspicions were confirmed, he was on the run or possibly dead. Mister Red Hair knew that. He was working for Marino.

I spent the next five hours checking the city records and Rugolo's own system to find some numbers. What I discovered made it seem like Janine had been padding certain costs on the jobs Marino had been involved with. For the last three years, Anselm Tijeras, Marino's relative on the city council, had taken a hand in every project Janine had managed. It seemed like an obvious payoff but probably nothing unusual. The question was: how had Marino been using his skim? He was a religious fanatic bankrolling a terror campaign with Pete and Janine's money. Janine must have figured it out and tried to fix it herself. Now she could be charged as an accessory.

I was ready to head back home. I had everything I needed to take this to Pete tomorrow. I had a strong feeling we were going to win this one.

As I entered Pete's office I adjusted my suit to make sure it was hanging right. "There's some news," I said.

"Where'd you get those bruises?"

"I pushed a little bit, I got what I deserved."

"I hope it was worth it," Pete said. "Everything in this business is a fight. That's why I needed you. I can't get down into the trenches the way I used to."

"Janine is having some trouble. She's been trying to handle it herself. That's why she hasn't been around."

"That must be why she hasn't been coming around."

"She's been working like a champ. If you look through this report I put together you'll see. She's going to need you to back her up to get out of this jam."

"You need to find her. Tell her I want to see her."

"She's been buying Marino Tijeras' pull with the city council and the Mexicans. The amount of money she's been knocking off shows that it was working. But Marino was knocking off money, too. That's where the trouble started."

"I wanted her to stick with my guys."

"That's the way it used to work, Pete. You aren't down in the trenches; Janine did what she had to do, what you would have done thirty years ago."

"She doesn't like to be told what to do. There's a thin line between pride and disloyalty."

"She's been working with Marino for a while. She pads his costs but he doesn't use the money for island trips or cars. He's a fanatical Catholic, he uses the money to fund a holy war. The cops are looking at him for these clinic bombings that have been going on. I think Janine figured it out and tried to cut him off; but Marino couldn't let it go. He must have been keeping records all the time, something he can use against her."

"I need to see her."

"I want to meet with her and explain what we know. The cops will take care of Marino. We should be able to fix this so nothing blows back on us."

"Janine is difficult, all she had to do was tell me. Go, find her and call me."

I stopped at a pay phone near the library. I wanted to call Springwood and see if Janine had been there. A hot, thin piercing strained in my thigh muscle. I twisted and my back was up against the phone. I scraped down towards the sidewalk, blinking my eyes in waves. Mister Red Hair held a syringe, he wiped his face and watched me. I saw the street broken like in the frames of a comic strip. He took me to his car and shut me in the trunk.

I awoke to darkness. It felt like we were on the highway. The car turned and I rattled inside that trunk for thirty minutes or so; then we stopped. We were in the wooded hills close to a spot I thought I recognized. Mister Red Hair was leading me down a tangled, foot worn path that ended at an inhospitable corner of Lake Guylin. The smell of the lake had grown worse over the years. Hot vapor puked off the swamp as Mister Red Hair set me down on a tree stump.

"Did Marino hire you?" I asked.

"That dumb thug doesn't run me."

"Are you one of those Christians? Do you want to be like Jesus or Noah or that other guy?"

"Abraham?"

"That guy in the movie, with the big beard." I tried to talk my head clear.

"Moses."

"Yeah. Did Marino drag Janine into the bombing plot?"

"Is that what Pete told you?" He waded out into the muck and started towing something in at the end of a rope.

"Pete hired me to watch out for his investments."

"Why do you think Marino is involved with those bombings?"

"I did the leg work!" I shouted.

He pulled a canoe up onto the bank. "You were at his place when the cops were there."

"I was eating some Mexican food."

"Did you see me there?" He asked.

"Fuck, no. I don't know who you are but you don't have anything to do with what is going on. You've been a fucking bee I can't brush off. What do you want with me?"

"What does Janine have to do with the bombings?"

"Nothing, I don't think," I said. He dropped the rope. He pulled a plastic bag and duct tape out of the canoe. He stared at me while massaging the plastic bag with his hands. "Do you work with Marino? Whatever you're after Pete can straighten this all out. He just hired me to try and keep Janine safe."

"I want the reward money," he said. He dropped the plastic bag.

"For what?"

"The reward money for Marino, from the FBI. I'm a private investigator, too."

"I just want to get my ass off the hook. I don't give a shit about the money. I was just supposed to check into Pete's investments and make sure Janine wasn't in trouble."

"I just needed to check you out. Maybe we can help each other."

He lifted me up. I found I could walk. I was still drugged but it all seemed to make sense. We could share what we knew and work together. If he wanted the money so bad I was more than glad to help him. He opened the car door and I stumbled into the passenger seat. He told me his name was Charlie. He decided I should call Pete and explain why I had cocked up and not called earlier. I agreed I shouldn't wait, Pete had to be nervous.

"Janine hired me to watch Marino for a week," Charlie said as we drove back to the city. "She wanted to retaliate. I wanted the reward money, so I took the case. We all need to meet up at Springwood tonight. That's where Marino is."

We arrived back at the library. "Call Pete like nothing happened. I'll grab Janine and we'll go to Springwood. Pick Pete up and give him the rundown on the way over. You can question Marino and make sure he doesn't have anything on Janine. Then I'll take him in."

"I'll do the best I can," I said.

Pete was in pain on the phone. He couldn't control the situation. He couldn't stand that Janine had gotten so tangled up. He thrived on her intensity but now he had no jurisdiction. I got him to agree to come with me to Springwood. I met him downstairs from his office, he seemed scattered. He was still carrying his briefcase. I told him the whole story but not what was waiting for us when we got to Springwood. I would finish it up when we were all together.

There were two cars parked by the model home. "There's her car, Janine is here." Pete got out and headed up the walk. Janine was standing in the front door. "How could you put me through this? Get over here," Pete shouted.

"Whatever you say." Janine looked at me and rolled her eyes.

"Calm down, Pete." I grabbed his shoulder but he pushed me away. He slapped Janine across the face.

"I told you I wouldn't let you get away from me," Pete said.

"What are you doing Pete?" I asked.

"That's the spirit, knucks, tell this pig to keep his hands off me." Janine sat down on the steps and lit a cigarette. "You never called the cops, Pete. I guess you figured out that if they heard my story they'd believe it."

"Not when they find out you've been stealing from me. Or how you've been cheating on me. I didn't say you could do that." I was holding onto Pete, he was shaking.

"This time I did it because I wanted to," Janine said.

"I don't understand, Pete. Here she is, she's all right," I said, relaxing my grip.

"Don't listen to what she says. I needed someone I could trust to find her." Pete looked around, Charlie was standing next to Janine's car. "Is that him, Janine? Watch me cut this guy's nuts off." Pete flipped open his briefcase. He ran clumsily toward the car. Charlie flashed the high beams on and I couldn't see him. Janine darted across the light and dashed something heavy across Pete's head. I didn't see the hit but I heard bone collapse with a thick pop, air gushed rapidly. Pete fell into the sewer ditch.

"He's finished. Crawl into that hole with him, you're next," Charlie said.

"This can't be right," I said.

Janine was hyperventilating, kneeling on the lawn. Charlie went to her, "It's over, he can't hurt you again." He kept saying it and I watched them in the shadows.

"There was something wrong between them," I said.

"You don't know anything," Charlie said. "You don't know what Pete has been doing to her, all the abuse and torture she's been through. You stupid jock, you really don't know."

"She seemed like a tough person, a little weird; I never thought about it," I said.

"I can't even talk about the things he did to her. It had to stop but she couldn't get out, he had control of everything, the money, the accounts. We started skimming from him, hiding it. He hired you because he finally had to admit he lost control. He knew you wouldn't ask any questions," Charlie said. He led me over to Janine's car and

I saw Marino stretched out in the backseat, dead. I leaned over and yanked the crucifix from around his neck.

"Can you still get the reward money if he's dead?" I asked.

"There's no reward money. Marino had discovered what we were doing. He threatened to go to Pete," Charlie said.

"He wasn't setting off bombs," I explained to myself.

"We could just go to the cops, Charlie," Janine said. "We could figure it out. He'll tell them whatever we say. You'd do that for us wouldn't you, knucks?"

"We have to keep that money. I'm sorry, man. You were working for a bad, bad guy." Charlie lifted Marino's body and put him in the ditch with Pete. "This is how it worked out, Janine. Everyone who knows will be dead and the cops will have to think it was a private beef. We have to go all the way."

"They're going to think I killed them?" I asked.

"I'm sorry, man," Charlie repeated.

Pete lurched up from the ditch as if he were on a wire, he tried to scream but only spit blood. He braced his forearm against Charlie's neck and threw him down. "I'll take care of him here, Janine. I have a shoebox full of screwdrivers back at the house for you," Pete hissed.

I jumped on Pete and he fell back. He flipped me over and wedged his knee into my chest. Pete tried to grab his briefcase, I saw a pistol inside just before Charlie kicked at it. I reached for the loose gun but Pete was standing over me. I felt blood on my neck. Charlie made a move but Pete grabbed the gun and unloaded the clip into my chest. Pete raised the pistol at Charlie but snapped off nothing but empties. Charlie tackled Pete and strangled him.

Charlie was kneeling beside me. "Hold on, sport. Maybe we can get you an ambulance. You won't say anything to the cops, will you? We can tell them Pete did all this."

"I know he shot me, man. I'm gone, finished. You get Janine away from here like you planned. Make them think I did this, it'll be easy. Thanks for not killing me back at the lake." I squeezed his hand.

"Hold on. We can fix you up. Stay with me," Charlie whispered.

I didn't say anything.